W9-CTF-004

Praise for Lauren Dane's
Reading Between the Lines

Rating: Five Hearts "This reviewer has been a fan of Ms. Dane's books since her first book was released, but she is still surprised that Ms. Dane's book can get even better than the last one. READING BETWEEN THE LINES is no exception, because it's her best so far"

~ *Loveromances*

Rating: Five Blue Ribbons "Lauren Dane intrigued me with this tale from the very first page."

~ *Romance Junkies*

Rating: Four and a half Hearts "This is a very exciting tale with some thrillingly suspenseful scenes and a very erotic love story. I doubt you will be able to put it down until the end."

~ *The Romance Studio*

Look for these titles by
Lauren Dane

Now Available:

The Chase Brothers Series
Giving Chase
Taking Chase
Chased
Making Chase

Cascadia Wolves Series
Wolf Unbound
Standoff

To Do List

Coming Soon:

Cascadia Wolves Series
Unexpected

Reading Between the Lines

Lauren Dane

A Samhain Publishing, Ltd. publication.

Samhain Publishing, Ltd.
577 Mulberry Street, Suite 1520
Macon, GA 31201
www.samhainpublishing.com

Reading Between the Lines
Copyright © 2008 by Lauren Dane
Print ISBN: 978-1-59998-834-4
Digital ISBN: 1-59998-672-8

Editing by Angela James
Cover by Anne Cain

This book is a work of fiction. The names, characters, places, and incidents are products of the writer's imagination or have been used fictitiously and are not to be construed as real. Any resemblance to persons, living or dead, actual events, locale or organizations is entirely coincidental.

All Rights Are Reserved. No part of this book may be used or reproduced in any manner whatsoever without written permission, except in the case of brief quotations embodied in critical articles and reviews.

First Samhain Publishing, Ltd. electronic publication: October 2007
First Samhain Publishing, Ltd. print publication: August 2008

Dedication

I had this class in college called The Mythic Image. I absolutely LOVED the subject—world mythology—even though jerky guy also took the class. Jerky guy was the crankiest woman hater I've ever met in person, which says a lot, let me tell you! Anyway, jerky guy used to get all offended if I wrote about goddesses. Which uh, hello, this class is about mythology, doofus, what do you think people would write about? In truth, his reaction just made me want to write about them more. With all the extra research I did to write the best papers possible to present to the class and annoy jerky guy, I learned a heck of a lot about Celtic mythology, which remains a favorite to this day. So I want to dedicate this story to jerky guy. Thanks, JG, for helping me find this amazing world filled with powerful women and strong, smart men.

And always to my dude, who keeps the monsters occupied with Pokémon and pudding so I can get work done.

The usual suspects: Angie, the whip wielder—thank you. My beta readers—thanks for always finding the time in your schedules to read for me and for petting my ego but not blowing sunshine up my skirt. Oh and Megan, for bringing the sunshine up my skirt phrase into my life because it rocks, lml.

Chapter One

Haley O'Brian scowled at her idiot co-worker as she stood, arms crossed, hip propped against the counter. "You did what?"

"I tripped over one of the paving stones just outside the ring. It came loose and the pouch with the scrolls inside was right there beneath." His hands came up defensively when he caught her facial expression. "Okay, so I know it's not *technically* legal, but *I* found the scrolls. Is it a crime to want to know what they say? Come on, in the name of science! When I saw they were Ogham, I knew you'd be the best person to translate."

"What is this, finders keepers? Are we in third grade now?" She exhaled violently. "First of all, that site is *cursed*. I told you that when I translated the symbols on the standing stones. Second of all, the best person to look at them is the governmental liaison. They've got their own scholars and they'll let us in on this if we go through them. You can't take antiquities from a site. *It's illegal*. For fuck's sake, Jerry, you know that. You're endangering the entire Foundation over this."

She pushed away from the counter and kept her eyes averted from the pouch on the table. God how she wanted to get her hands on those scrolls! But if you took shortcuts in their profession, it got around and you didn't get grants. No grants, no work. No work and she'd be using her shiny degree at Copy

9

Cafeteria for minimum wage.

And anyway, despite her modern upbringing, her grandmother was a witch. *Or something.* Haley didn't quite know what but it involved magic and she'd just gotten around to admitting she'd been too chicken to really ask.

Haley's parents may have disdained what they said was her gran's *superstition* but that ring of stones lay heavy with vengeful magic. The symbols were a curse to keep something in. It seemed wrong to break the law to read the scrolls on a lie, like giving in to whatever maliciousness the site was bound by. It wasn't superstitious to be smart. No way. She was calling Conall and not because the very sight of him made her tingly in all the right places either. *Uh uh.*

"Haley, we might never get to see them if you tell the liaison," Jerry whined.

She waved him away impatiently, annoyed at him over the scrolls and for interrupting the beginnings of a very salacious fantasy about the sexy Conall Shaunessey. "Jerry, I'm not going to do it. And if I don't you're screwed because I'm the best you've got. Anyone else with my skills will turn your ass in. You signed the contract. I'm a board member and I say tell the damned liaison. You're putting the scrolls back, right now. And then you'll call him from the site."

She saw the calculation on his face and wanted to groan aloud.

"I can't believe you're going to play goody-goody on this. But okay." He held his hands up again hastily as she moved toward him, wanting to smack him upside his head. "I'll take it back. But you have to come with me. You make the call and go with Shaunessey when he comes to take the scrolls. That way you can push your way into the room when they're translated."

It wasn't like she didn't want to take a gander at the

scrolls—she did. They called to her. She wanted to *know* what was on them. Having that pouch there within reach, knowing no one had read them in centuries ate away at her.

"Okay, let's go. Maybe I can look at them at the site before the liaison gets there."

He jumped up, grabbing the bag before heading out the door as she followed in his wake.

After a short walk through a prototypical sunny forest glade, the trees opened up and she saw the ring. The stones nearly sang in the sunlight shafting over their gray surface. Cursed or not, it was a place thick with magic and Haley's own responded in kind, surging through her as like recognized like.

As she stood there, a sense of expectancy hung in the air. Something big lay in the shadows of the future, coiled up and ready to spring. A shiver passed through Haley as she attempted to shake the feeling off.

Haley knew what she needed to do was to give in and go visit her grandmother and get some answers. She responded deeply to the space and it seemed foolhardy not to ask. Nearly as stupid as the fight that drove her from her grandmother's house six months prior.

She realized that Jerry had been babbling as they'd been walking. Given his predilection for haring off on wild schemes, she figured she should at least pay half attention or it could be disastrous.

The circle of stones stood there, cold and dangerous. They brought a feel of dread to the glade, which would have been a damp, but otherwise lovely spot but for those gray stones looming in their midst.

As they'd approached, all other sound died out. No birds, no flicker of the leaves dancing against each other in the breeze. The magic of the circle hung heavy and humid. Even those

11

without any magical gifts had eschewed the spot, no one had done any real investigation of the standing circle despite its age. Haley knew, given the samples they'd taken and the general state of the stones and carving, that it was roughly a thousand years old. Stunning really, to think of anything that old being avoided for so long. It made Haley glad she didn't need to be on site most of the time.

"Here's the spot where I found the pouch." Jerry pointed to a very smooth stone right inside the northern edge of the circle of stones. She bent and looked, noted the small amount of wear from a prying tool and rolled her eyes up to glare at him.

Sheepishly, he handed her the pouch. The magic spilled through Haley, as dark as the magic in the stones themselves. But there was something else in the leather bag. Something vibrant. The pouch wasn't in the best shape and after she'd peeked and verified the scrolls did indeed have Ogham script on them, she'd decided not to take them out until they were in a lab. Jerry may have been an ass but she knew he'd have taken great care when he removed them. Still, best not to take chances and have the parchment fall apart.

Satisfied that he'd obeyed at least the spirit of her instructions, she placed the container holding the pouch near the spot where the stone had been dug up and pushed aside— *yeah right he tripped over the rock and it just came up*—and pulled out her cell phone to call Conall, the liaison the Irish government had assigned to the site.

Conall Shaunessey looked at the display screen on his phone and a whisper of a long forgotten emotion slid outside his reach. It was the American Irishwoman from the Foundation. Haley.

"Conall Shaunessey," he answered.

"Hi, Conall, it's Haley O'Brian from the Foundation. We've found something out here that I think you should take a look at."

Finally, she'd found the bleeding scrolls. He shoved the thought down. "Well isn't that interesting? What is it?"

"Scrolls. They're in a leather pouch. I don't want to pull them out though. The pouch looks to be centuries old. I'd prefer to get them in a better environment than out here. I don't want the paper to disintegrate. I did take a peek, without removing them completely or unrolling them. Looks like Ogham."

"Sounds like quite a find. I'll be out with my team in an hour. Thank you, Haley." He'd known she'd call, knew she'd be honorable and not break the law. Another positive in his favor.

He hung up and arranged for photographers and other staff to get out there and log the site. Of course he knew the contents and geography of that damned ring like the back of his hand but he couldn't forget his position. The find would need to be recorded for historical posterity.

An hour later, he strolled through the glade and tried not to glare at the stones. Inside him, there was a faint stirring but he focused on her instead.

He'd always known it would take the right person to find the scrolls. The right witch with that touch of Faerie magic to end the damnable curse and let his soul free. Each time he'd been born into a new body but as half a person, his soul firmly rooted in the cage of those stones. And each time he died as the scrolls went undiscovered, only to go through the same process over and over again.

But when Haley O'Brian had walked into his office, tall and lithe, red hair the color of the last gasp of the sunset, eyes a bright, curious mossy-green, he felt real hope. Or as close to feeling as he'd done in centuries. As well as a whisper of desire.

Her skin was touchable, creamy and pale, a dash of freckles punctuated her nose and cheeks. So Irish he couldn't help but grin at her. He felt her magic crackle around her and tasted the Fae in it. Her immediate fascination with the site was the last clue and he knew it was finally time. More than that, he knew she was his. Finding the patience to survive the last months waiting for her to find the ring and then the scrolls would have been torture but he supposed it was one time he could actually be thankful the curse robbed him of emotion. She was the one and the curse would be lifted.

As he came upon the stones, he saw her standing there, sketchbook in her hands, bottom lip caught between her teeth in concentration.

"Hoy!" he called out as he approached with his people. She looked up at him and as always, it was as if she saw right through him. That jolt of recognition shot to his toes. And to other parts like his cock, which always stirred to life in her presence, not like he'd be able to do anything with it until after she broke the curse.

She waved a hand at him in greeting as he reached her. "Hi there. It's here." She motioned to the rock and the leather pouch.

With calm efficiency, he ordered his crew to get started. He couldn't touch the scrolls though. But that wasn't a problem, he knew damned well Haley would want to.

"This is your prize. Why don't you bag it up and bring it back? I'm guessing you'd like to be the one to translate?"

Her eyes lit, followed by a very sexy grin. "Of course. You know I would. Thank you. But," she hesitated, "I'm certainly not the only person who can translate Ogham."

She was so deliciously earnest he wanted to eat her up. He *would* eat her up. "Ah, Haley, but this is your project and don't be so modest. Your reputation is the reason your proposal was approved to handle this site to begin with. Now come. I'll let you bag it up and we'll get to my lab to start work. Do you have the time now?"

"Yes, yes. Oh and thank you."

She bent and carefully slid the pouch into a bag after it'd been photographed by his people. They headed out of the glade and back out toward the vehicles.

"I'll be sure Ms. O'Brian gets back to her flat," Conall called to the other man from the Foundation over his shoulder. He wanted to make it clear that the other man was most definitely not invited.

After feeling nothing for so long, being around Haley was like a balm to his senses. He actually admired her. The way she moved, economical but graceful as she navigated the trail and got into his car. Even the small things like the lilt to her voice, the sweet honey of her accent, pulled long forgotten memories from him at what it was like to be moved by a woman. He couldn't wait to hear her speak the spell aloud to free his soul.

Oh man, did she have a thing for the ever-so-delicious Conall Shaunessey. What man had a right to look so good? Black hair that barely brushed his collar, piercing blue eyes with sooty lashes. Long and lean, he stood at six-and-a-half feet easy and she absolutely adored the relaxed attitude he had. Jeans and wool sweaters worked on him. And the accent? Every time he spoke he made her wet. Thick, velvet Irish, the cadence was poetic.

On top of all that, he was letting her translate. He was too good to be true and really, if he did not ask her out to dinner soon she'd take matters into her own hands. Um, well she had, many times, but this time she'd ask him out herself, no matter what her mother would say about women waiting for the man to make the first move. Then he could be the one to take matters into his hands. *Heh.*

She snuck looks at him as he drove, his grip easy on the steering wheel. Nice hands, long fingers. She squirmed in her seat a bit as she wondered what they'd feel like against her naked skin.

Focus, Haley!

They headed back into the larger city where his office and lab resided. The drive would take about forty-five minutes and the way he smelled would surely drive her insane.

"So, you'd mentioned your family was Irish?"

She turned to face him. "Yes. My mother was born in Los Angeles but my maternal grandparents are from Dublin. They were in a car accident and died when my mother was in her twenties. My father was born here and his mother, my gran, still lives here. In Kerry actually."

"I'm sorry about your grandparents. I thought I recognized that wee bit of an accent when you use place names." He smiled. "How did your parents end up in America then?"

"My maternal grandfather was an artist. He made all kinds of pottery and my grandparents lived in Los Angeles half the year and here the other half. My mother was born when they were in the US. She decided to stay when it was time for school. She's a chemist. That's where she met my father. He was a visiting fellow at UC Berkeley."

"Both parents are scientists?"

She nodded. "Yep. Big fun in the O'Brian household was robot wars and mold experiments. I still like robot wars. My father works for a big tech company now."

"Robot wars?"

"Oh yes! My dad and I would build these robots from other things, remote control cars and toys, that sort of thing. And then we'd set them on each other in battle."

Startled, he laughed at the look on her face. A sort of feral joy. Her eyes danced with amusement. "Well now. You'll have to teach me that one, it sounds like fabulous fun."

"I'd love to. And it is. Just have a fire extinguisher on hand. So obviously you were raised here?"

"Yes. My father is a school teacher and my mother is the parish secretary. They live in Cork near my sister and younger brother. I'm not very close to them though. Haven't seen any of them in several years." Which was his fault, he knew. It was easier all around when he dropped away from his family when he came of age.

He pulled the car around into his spot and they got out. She quickly grabbed the bin with the pouch and scrolls inside and followed him into the building.

The faintest anticipation tickled at him. For so long he'd felt only shadows of real emotion. Without his soul he was unable to feel real love, real happiness. People always thought he was overly serious and he knew every one of his mothers had yearned for his real love and laughter but in time, he'd faked it the best he could. One small blessing of the curse was that he'd been born over and over with the memories of what he'd been before. It was those memories of feeling that kept him from becoming a sociopath. He didn't even feel guilt about it, didn't even have that left. It made things easier. In truth, the worst part was the lack of any sort of true connection to anyone else. Haley had been the first woman in many lifetimes that he'd actually had a physical reaction to and an actual yearning for. Still, he couldn't have sex either and goddess he missed that.

He did plan to change that situation right after Haley read the scrolls and freed him.

He flipped on the lights and motioned her into the lab adjoining his office. "Do you object to getting started now?"

With a soft snort, she rolled her eyes and put the bin on a table, turning to remove her jacket and hang it on the rack.

"All right then. I'll manage to get some food in here. Do you need anything else?" he asked.

She blushed. "Um, I'm a bit of a control freak about translation. My gran, well, she taught me to approach the Ogham with respect for its magic and history. I hope you're not offended by a bit of ritual."

He stood back and bowed. "Of course not. I respect that you approach our history with the reverence it deserves. As for ritual and magic?" He shrugged. "It makes sense."

She opened her bag and pulled out a smaller, velvet pouch and placed it on the table next to the leather pouch the scrolls resided in. He kept back, he had to remain utterly uninvolved in the translation or the curse would not be broken.

He watched as she washed her hands and the scent of laurel and rosemary rose as she lit incense. Ahhh, a bit of cinnamon too.

Her lips moved as she spoke an entreaty for protection and wisdom and turned to him, smiling.

"I hope you don't mind the smell. I make the incense myself."

Interesting for the daughter of scientists to make her own incense for divination and wisdom. He'd ask her about it later. After he was whole again.

"No. Not a problem. I like it."

She laid out a sheet of cotton and put on gloves. "I wish I

didn't have to wear gloves." Her voice was wistful but her face fell into an intent mask as she pulled the first scroll out and unrolled it carefully.

"Can you snap a few photographs of this for me please?" she asked, distracted as she began to examine the script. "Beautiful," she breathed.

He moved behind her with his digital camera and took photos for her. He'd been bound as Ninane had written the curse originally. In his blood. He'd never seen it up close, only felt the tentacles of the magic as it rent his soul from his body. A faint memory of how he'd felt then came to him, not the same as feeling it but the closest thing he had.

After several hours she'd written down the translation of the first scroll and moved to the second. She was so focused, she'd refused any food, only drinking tea in several quick gulps and moving back to the table to work.

He waited. The sun went down as she worked. The building emptied out until it was only the two of them left.

"All right, I think I can give a bare translation."

Nodding, he willed her to say it aloud.

"I'm sorry it took me so long. It's actually not that complicated but the symbols have faded and I needed to piece it all together to get context. It appears to be a binding spell. *Nuin* here, the ash, it's in several places. Thing is, whoever wrote this, well, it's a twisting of the magic into something very wrong."

More nodding. Thank the goddess she saw that.

"Okay, so you know how it works. It's not going to translate into what we'd think of as grammatically correct language, it's more the language of feeling and magic. Loosely then: Bound by stone around your soul, bound by earth and circle glen, bound until the way is made, through word, by act, rent asunder,

19

heart and soul."

The air stirred then, cool first and then very warm. Haley felt the intent in what she'd just translated, wondering too late what the hell she'd done.

Spinning to face Conall, her eyes widened as she took him in, his head cast back, mouth open, a deep green light spilled out, followed by a pale one, seemingly shining from within him.

"Conall?"

He fell to his knees, knocking over a plant, sending dirt everywhere. In it, he traced an X with a line dissecting the vertical center. *Koad*, the grove. Wisdom gained through living and seeing truth where once there was illusion.

She'd backed up, the edge of the work table cutting into the small of her back. Her hand pressed over her thundering heart.

He slowly looked up, tears shining in his eyes. "Thank you. Goddess be praised, thank you, Haley, for freeing my soul."

She couldn't even speak, panic closed her throat. Had that shadow sprung? Was this it? What the fuck had she done?

Easing up from his knees, Conall held out his hands. "I pose you no threat. The spell that bound my soul in that ring was evil, I am not. Look at me and know the truth. You've the magic to divine that yourself."

The fear ebbed a bit. "What. The. Fuck. Is. Happening?" She sensed the truth of his words. He hadn't felt evil. Not before whatever had happened and not now. Still, she wasn't just going to shrug her shoulders and walk away without some questions answered.

"Can I take you to dinner? Down the local pub. Loads of people around. I've been unable to enjoy a meal for more years than I can count. I'll answer all your questions, I make my vow to you."

Sighing, she took his measure before nodding shortly. "You bet you will. I won't hesitate to kick you square in the balls if you try to mess with me. And you're paying."

He smiled. "I have no doubt you would and of course I'm paying."

Chapter Two

Emotions! He'd forgotten the everyday wonder of just existing. He'd have time to be pissed off at Ninane later. But for the moment, he sat in a pub, enjoying the sensory feast before him. Truly able to appreciate eating dinner with a beautiful woman—*his woman*. The same woman who'd freed him from the prison his existence had been.

She smelled good too. The beer smelled good, food tasted good. He enjoyed it, enjoyed her. How he'd missed that subtle back and forth with a woman, each seducing the other. She was wary, yes, but thankfully not afraid. And with each breath he took, his magic returned like an old friend, filling each cell slowly.

"Okay, you've had your Guinness, you've eaten enough for three men, now you have a story to tell. Who the hell are you? Tell me. All of it."

"I am Conall macCormac. I truly was born thirty-seven years ago to Billy and Janet Shaunessey, as I said. But to answer your real question, I am *Daoine Sidhe* and I was cursed by a very nasty sorceress because I wouldn't betray my queen. She stole my soul and killed me and I've been reborn nine times. Each lifetime, I've been without emotion, without connection. I've been unable to love my family of birth and I've been unable to contact my original family." Suddenly the depth of emptiness he'd been living with hit him square in the gut and he had to pause and take a few swallows of Guinness.

Haley reached across the table and touched the back of his hand, a butterfly of a touch and their magic flared, bringing a gasp to her lips.

"I'm sorry. I can't imagine. You lost so much. I take it my translation and recital of the scrolls did something to undo it? Why did you wait all this time?"

"Curses are dark magic. Performing dark magic costs the person who does it. Because she had a murder on her hands as it was, she crafted the curse in such a way that it could be undone so as not to damn herself totally. But to undo the curse, I was unable to help in any way, not direct or suggest. And the right person had to translate. A witch with a touch of Fae in her blood."

Startled, she blinked quickly. "What?"

He laughed. "The Ogham is more than symbols and words. Magic carries intent and flavor. You have Faerie magic in your blood, Haley. You know that."

"I know that? What? You're telling me I'm a Faerie?"

He leaned in and took a deep whiff of her. "Mmmm, yes. Not too far from the hill, maybe a generation or two. Not your parents but perhaps your grandfather? Don't tell me you don't know."

The day just kept throwing more and more her way. The weight of it sent her reeling, trying to grasp it all but failing as it slipped through her fingers. Her grandmother's words the last time Haley visited came back to her. She knew she had magic, that wasn't in doubt, but a Faerie?

She stood up and grabbed her bag. "I have to talk to my grandmother. I can't believe this day," she mumbled, grabbing his pint glass and draining it. At least the warmth of the alcohol

23

numbed the impending fall into total insanity.

He joined her, looming above her, dominating the space with his sexual lure, with the way he smelled. Her mouth watered to taste him. Oh, this was bad.

Tucking her hand into the crook of his arm, he propelled her toward the door and out onto the quiet street beyond. "After you come back to my flat." His eyes seemed to glow when she looked up into them, stealing her good sense. He continued, "I need to contact my family too. Nine hundred years without any word, they'll likely have believed me dead. But I don't have all my magic back yet so I can't get into the hill. Still, I can think of a few ways to pass the time."

She looked into his eyes and a wave of desire so strong she might have stumbled had she not been leaning on him, rushed over her. "I...are you propositioning me?"

So close, his lips hovered above hers, his breath against her mouth, shivers blanketed her as her nipples tightened. "Haley, I want to make love to you. And then I want to fuck you. Do you know how I knew you were the one to free my soul? When you walked into my office that first day and my cock jolted to life. You're the only woman who's done that in the entire time I lived with the curse. I want you. I want to touch you. Taste you. I want to feel you from deep inside."

His lips brushed over hers then and her body warmed, tightened and loosened all at once. Insanity, that's what it was. Hormonal insanity because she hadn't had sex in eight months. All kinds of crazy had descended into her life and her hormones thought they'd take her on a holiday. And it sounded pretty damned good right about then.

"I really need to talk to my grandmother. This is all so bizarre." Her eyes remained halfway closed, his body against hers.

"Haley, it's half-past eleven. You said she lives in Kerry, that's two hours away in the daylight. She'll be sleeping until the morning, I'm sure. Come, while away the darkness with me in my bed. I can feel your nipples through your shirt. I know you want me too."

Oh good heavens, she was going to have sex with a formerly cursed Faerie. A stranger who was a formerly cursed Faerie. Well, technically, she'd known him for the last six months, had certainly been attracted to him since that first meeting and she did have a very strong and accurate sense of people. Lawd, talking herself into fucking a handsome man, she needed to get out more.

"Would you prefer your flat? Would that make you feel safer? You know I'd not harm you, don't you?" His thumb slid down the line of her jaw.

Her flat did have some magical warding her gran had performed when Haley'd first moved in, and her bed was nice and big.

"How far are you from here?" God, she had to be crazy to even consider this.

That smile again, wicked, wicked man. "I'm only down the road a piece. My car is at my office. If we walk back there, I can have us to my flat in ten minutes."

"I'm just the other way, probably the same amount of time. Let's go there."

His hand at the small of her back, he steered her toward the lot where he'd parked. "I bet your flat smells like you. Lilac, that's very nice."

"Were you this full of it before the curse?"

He laughed and squeezed her to his side briefly. "My mother used to tell me so. But in all honesty, Haley, I mean it. I do want you, very much. Not just because I've not lain with a

25

woman in centuries, but because you're you. You stir things deep within me."

Oh boy, was she ever a horny fool. But his words moved her despite knowing she was a fool.

The drive to her apartment was relatively fast and before she knew it, they stood at her door while she fumbled through her bag for her keys. Quickly unlocking the deadbolt, they entered and she closed the door behind her. Silence fell between them again as the air grew heavy with promise.

Eyes closed, he took a deep breath. "Yes, it does smell like you. And magic. Not only yours though. Ahh." He opened his eyes and watched as she hung up her coat and bag and toed off her shoes. "Fae magic. Female. Your grandmother set the wards here, didn't she?"

"How can you tell?"

He tossed his jacket up on the rack and followed suit with his shoes, leaving them next to hers at the door. "You can't tell a magic's signature?" He stalked to her, encircling her waist and pulling her body against his.

"I can tell if there's magic somewhere and usually if it's right or wrong. But I don't think I've ever really focused on different signatures before."

"Okay, we'll talk about all this. *After.* Because right now I need to see you naked and beneath me."

"Behind me. My bedroom is just behind." Her hand waved somewhat uselessly in the general direction of her room as he moved her toward it and through the door, kicking it shut behind them.

With the moon shining through the big bay windows, he leaned in and finally kissed her. Not simply a brush of lips but a kiss that rocked her very foundations.

Her fingers dug into the muscles of his upper arms as she held on and opened herself to his plunder of her mouth. A masterful possession of a kiss, his tongue, confident and sensual, stroked along hers, tickled the roof of her mouth, the insides of her cheeks, pulling back only to be replaced by the sharp nip of teeth over the flesh of her bottom lip.

On and on it went until she lost all sense of time and everything simply was right there in that room, within the circle of his arms. His taste wove a spell over her system—the earthy tang of Guinness, the acid of the malt vinegar from the fish and chips and beneath that, some elemental spice that she knew was his alone.

A deep moan came from him, vibrating through his body and against hers. He broke the kiss and looked into her face. "You taste so good. Let me taste the rest of you."

After he released her from his embrace, she managed to get her lust-stunned fingers to work to grab the hem of her sweater and yank it over her head. She wished she'd worn something a bit more sexy than the utilitarian white cotton bra but it was too late for that.

Apparently he was just fine with utilitarian. When she looked up at him, that wicked smile had returned and he'd pulled his own sweater off. Lean, hard muscle banded his chest and upper body. His belly was flat and a light arrow of hair pointed from his navel to beneath the waist of the pants he had on.

In for a penny. She quickly unbuttoned and unzipped her jeans and kicked them off. At least the panties were sexy. Not by design. All the regular cotton bikini panties she usually wore were currently in her laundry basket so she only had her "back of the panty drawer" supply left. The thong-style panties her ex-boyfriend had given her some years before on Valentine's Day.

"Aren't you a bundle of contradictions?" His voice was lazy as he reached down and divested himself of his pants and then the boxer briefs he'd been wearing. The socks were gone in moments and when he turned his attention back to her, he was totally naked and very happy to be there.

"Show me, Haley. Let me see all of you." His hands fisted at his sides as he heaved in breath.

Reaching up quickly, she popped the catch on the bra and let it fall then bent to get rid of the panties. By the time she looked up, he'd moved to her.

"Every bit as beautiful as I'd thought." Bending his head, he traced his tongue over the freckles on her shoulders. His hands skimmed over her collarbone and clever fingertips danced over hardened nipples.

"Such beautiful skin. Irishwomen, I love them. Pale like moonlight. Soft. Your nipples, mmm." He rolled them between his thumb and forefinger for emphasis. "A very pretty shade of cinnamon."

His hands left her to pull the coverlet back and pushed her to the mattress carefully. Words escaped her as she took in the focus on his face, the greed with which he looked at her.

He was long, tall, rangy and yet, whip-strong and hard. An interesting build for an academic. No tattoos but there seemed to be a whisper of something on his right biceps and up his shoulder. Tawny skin. She'd thought him paler but unclothed she realized he wasn't pale like her at all, his skin almost had a golden tone to it.

She'd meant to ask him about his shoulder but his lips found her nipple and the thought skittered away, replaced by the warm tug and lick that shot straight to her clit.

When she reached down to take his cock into her hands, he moved back, separating from her nipple with a wet *pop*. "No. It's been so long. If you touch me, I'll come right away. Let me make you ready first."

Ready? Hello, she was so wet her thighs were sticky. She would have been embarrassed if thoughts of what his idea of ready might entail hadn't consumed her last two working brain cells.

And even those two stopped working once his body settled between her thighs and his hands pushed her legs apart as they slid up the sensitive flesh, stopping at her pussy.

Thumbs parted her to his gaze and she shivered as cool air hit the heated, wet folds of her cunt.

Want thrust into Conall with force, so deep and massive his hands shook. It wasn't just that he hadn't been with a woman for so long, it was *this* woman and the effect she had on him. Every inch of his skin felt over-sensitized, especially where her hands lay on him, the tips of her fingers digging into his shoulders. He wanted to crawl inside her and never leave. The scent of her body drove him to distraction. And when he leaned in and took a long lick, the taste of her, her essence, laced with magic, arced up his spine.

His tongue flicked over the swollen, slick bundle of her clit and the sound of her strangled gasp caught him in its grasp. He wrestled with his need, attempting to control feelings he hadn't had in a very long time.

Arching her back, she pressed her pussy to him, silently begging him for more. He gave her more. Bringing her up over and over, a hair's breadth from climax, and backing off a beat or two only to drive her up again. Each cry and sob fed his need as her body slickened more, swelled, readied for his cock.

"Please! Conall, please let me come," she begged.

"As you wish," he spoke against her before sucking her clit gently between his teeth and pressing two fingers deep into her pussy.

The magic and energy of her orgasm wound around him and filled him up, giving his renewal a boost. The mark on his shoulder and biceps stung and the tips of his ears tingled.

He kissed a trail up her body as he moved up, reaching down to angle himself at the entrance of her pussy.

"Wait. Condom. I have some in the bathroom."

Flexing his hips, the head of his cock slid into her as he caught her gaze. "Don't need one. As a human without a soul, I was infertile and impotent. I haven't had sex in nine hundred years. And as a Fae again, I control my fertility. I won't impregnate you." *Yet.* Certainly not until he dealt with his family and he and Haley had discussed it.

Her breath caught but he held himself in place, waiting for her okay before he filled her totally. She nodded and, relieved, he pressed deep into her, nearly coming on the spot at how good the embrace of her cunt felt wrapped around his cock.

"Great Mother," he stuttered as he began to pull out and then press back into her body again, setting a sweet, agonizingly delicious rhythm.

Haley felt her magic respond to his, felt his react to hers. It was momentous, this joining. She should have stopped to think about it, it wasn't like her to simply jump into things without thinking, but all her body wanted was him. All her mind wanted and damn it, all her heart seemed to want. It wasn't just sex. Wasn't just a-fucking-mazing sex. There was something between her and Conall, something a lot deeper than anything she'd ever experienced before.

Hard, smooth skin tantalized her palms and fingers as she stroked over his naked body, needing to touch him. She wrapped her thighs around his waist, taking him deeper, loving the way the blue of his eyes deepened in response.

His hair was like ebony silk against her skin and that's when she noticed it was longer. His facial features were the same, his eyes a bit deeper blue, cheeks a bit sharper, but his hair had grown a good three inches and the shadow on his upper arm was now a blue-tinged tattoo. Brushing his hair back, she saw the top of his ears had taken a bit of a point.

"Conall, your hair, your ears, what's happening?"

"My soul self is returning." His words were a gasp as he quickened his pace, plunging deep and hard into her body as her own responded, her hips rolling to meet his thrusts.

"I'm Fae, my ears will return to their pointed shape. When she took my soul, my hair was waist long. My tribal marking," he turned to look at his shoulder and then back to her, "is returning as well. Joining with you has aided my magic's full return."

He kissed her hard, even as he continued to fuck deep into her. She tasted herself, her magic and his too. The combination set her on fire.

"I'm so close. Give me another, sweet Irish witch. I want to feel your pussy come around my cock." He changed his angle, grinding the length of his cock against her clit each time he drove into her. The friction was delicious and she felt another orgasm begin to build at the base of her spine.

Over and over again, incremental, inexorable, he drove her up until it burst over her with sweet, sharp pleasure. Her eyes blurred, as she looked up into his and heard his intake of breath, felt the jerk of his cock deep inside her as he came, flooding her body with his magic.

CB

When Haley woke in a tangle of warm limbs, she couldn't help the smile that came to her lips. Didn't want to. Her night with Conall hadn't provided much sleep but her muscles, which should have been sore, were loose and satisfied.

She turned to look at him and quite liked the transformation. His hair covered them both. The blue markings on his shoulder and wrapping around his biceps were very sexy. His body hadn't changed but she felt the metaphysical difference right off. The air between them hung heavy with sex and magic. She wasn't a virgin by any stretch of the imagination but never, even in longer term relationships, had she felt so *connected* to anyone. It wasn't just that they both had magic, but that their magic was unified in some sense, tied together.

She didn't know what the future would bring, but for that moment, she let herself enjoy it.

His eyes fluttered open and his sexy-wicked smile curved his lips. Unable not to, she leaned in and kissed him. She'd meant for it to be quick but he took over and was very thorough before he released her.

"Good morning, Irish witch. And how are you today?" Sitting, he reached up over his head to stretch and Haley watched the subtle play of his muscles as he did.

"Mmm, very satisfied. And you?"

He kissed her again, hard and fast. "Very nice answer. I feel good. My magic is back, all of it. I need to go to the hill today."

Suddenly the huge differences between them settled into her brain. Regret sliced through her, even though she was happy he'd be reunited with his family.

It must have shown on her face because he pulled her into his lap, facing him. She had no choice but to wrap her legs around him and let him bring her close.

"Haley? What is it, love?"

"Nothing. I'm happy you'll be reunited with your people. Living apart from them for all this time, well, I can't imagine the isolation."

"Yes. Fae are big on family. I've missed my sisters growing up, and my brother Riordan who was my closest mate. I've got three. I expect at least a few of them will have married, possibly even mated by now. They're going to love you."

"Me? You're taking me?"

He stilled, cocking his head. "Did you think I'd fuck and run? Did you think last night was just bedsport?"

"I don't know!" She tried to wriggle free but he held her to him.

"Haley, I've wanted you since the first time I saw you. I *knew* you. And after last night, my magic knows yours too. Can't you feel it? The connection between us? That's not *I-like-you* connection, that's heart-and-soul connection. That's rare. You do realize that?"

"What are you saying?" she whispered.

"Oh, sweet witch, I'm saying you're my woman as assuredly as I'm your man. When my family meets you, it'll be as my woman, as the mate of my soul. Surely you can feel the metaphysical bond between us?"

"Oy. I'm your magical mate? Like in some romance novel?"

He laughed and kissed the tip of her nose. "I don't know. I've never read one. Do they have sex in them?"

She rolled her eyes. "Some. But back to the question at hand."

"For some things there are words, explanations. The scientist in you knows that. But for others, it's all here." He kissed her chest, above her heart. "You *know* some things, even without the words to express them, you know them. Like the Ogham. The closest word is alphabet but you know it's more than that. If you were all human, I'm sure I'd still be attracted to you, still want you and want to be with you. But you're *more*. You're Fae and your magic and mine resonate, as our hearts do and now our souls. You have an old soul, Haley."

Haley blew out a breath. "So like this is a Faerie gig? The mate thing? Only one person in the whole world is your other half or whatever? What happens if you never meet them? Are you single forever?"

"No. Well, it is a Fae thing, yes. But it's rare, as I said. In most cases Fae are like humans. They meet someone and fall in love and share their lives with someone. A mate bond is unique. I don't know the statistics, but less than one in four. My parents are mated but no one else in my family has a mate although there are loads of marriages and kids. Or they didn't when I was taken from them." He took her hand, kissing her knuckles. "What you and I have is a miracle, Haley."

Her heart softened. The man was so charming he was an absolute menace.

"I'm guessing your grandmother will have something to say about all this as well. Shall we go see her first and then head to the hill?"

"You want to meet my gran?" Her voice squeaked at that thought. "My grandmother isn't some sweet old matron who'll make tea, you know. She's formidable. Sharp. She's going to give you the third degree and expect you to answer every question fully. It'll be like the scariest interrogation you've ever seen on television. Only she's the bad cop with better hair. And," she hesitated, "well you know there are a lot of unanswered questions so she's going to be very personal and possibly hostile."

He grinned. "I look forward to meeting another of The Gentry. Come on. You shower and I'm going back to my flat to grab a bag. I'll be back here in a few minutes. Now that I don't need to drive, it makes things much simpler." He stood and put her down gently. "You do want to come with me to meet my family, don't you? I'm not imagining this thing between us?"

The look on his face was so vulnerable for a quick moment all her defenses against him simply crumbled. "God, you're totally irresistible aren't you? I'm in so much trouble."

He winked. "It's the best kind of trouble, having a man who adores you and plans to fuck you and spoil you until you have not a single want."

He threw her off balance. Her senses were at war with her brain and common sense. Never in her life had she been so tempted to toss aside ration and embrace simply feeling. And yet she did. "I can't be gone too long. I do have a job, you know. But I'll take a few days and we can re-evaluate what the next steps will be. You sure you don't want to shower here. With me?"

"Temptress. Come on with you. Get yourself ready. I'll be back. We have loads to do today and then we can take our time in the bath and the bed after we've done it all."

A quick kiss to the tip of her nose and he was gone, leaving her with rubber knees and out of breath.

"Holy shit. He spelled himself out of here."

Pushing away the utter unreality of it all, Haley blew out a breath and headed for the shower.

Chapter Three

Conall tried not to look at Haley overlong. Each time he did, the need for her crept back into his system and made him shake. That tousled cap of red curls, the milky-pale skin, the freckles and pixie nose. He loved the way she looked. The combination of her features, a mishmash of so many elements, didn't make her a great beauty, but it made her striking. She was tall for a human woman, probably the Fae in her blood. Long legs, high, tight ass and breasts that made his hands itch to touch and his mouth water to taste. Not big—on the small side for his usual tastes. Barely a B cup but with nipples so sensitive he'd made her come just from licking and sucking on them.

"What's that grin for? You're making me nervous." She looked at him quickly before putting her eyes back on the road. She'd insisted they drive to her grandmother's home in Kerry. Totally unnecessary, he could have simply sifted them there in a matter of moments, but he'd indulged her. He knew she had a lot to process and wanted to give her some time.

"Thinking about your nipples and how I made you come without even touching your clit."

She blushed prettily. "Oh. Well. That's a new one for me. Can't say anyone's ever made me come that way."

"Good. Are you well? Hungry? Thirsty?"

"I'd kill for a latte. Tea is fine and all, I grew up with it, but I miss my chai lattes in the morning. I don't suppose there're Starbucks at your house? Hill? Barrow?"

"No. But you don't need one. You've got me. And it's a *Sithein*. The inside, where we live is the *Brugh*. You'll see. Here." He reached toward her and handed her a steaming cup.

She sniffed it carefully and sighed. "Get out of here!" She took a sip and groaned in a way that made his jeans tight. "How'd you know what to make it taste like?"

"I've always been reborn here in Ireland, but I have traveled to other countries and there are coffeehouses in Dublin and the bigger cities. I've even been to Starbucks a time or two."

"Why didn't you try to get back home? I mean, even without telling them of the curse, they'd have known you were alive. And oh, come to think of it, do you always get reborn being all hot and stuff?"

He laughed. "Thank you, Irish witch. Yes, I'm born looking the same in general time and again but as you've seen, my appearance changed a bit once I got my magic back. As for the other, I've been unable to find the entrance to the hill without my magic. I've not known my way home until last night when my magic returned in full. The door wouldn't have opened for me anyway. It would only recognize me when my tribal mark was alive."

She took another sip before putting it in the cup holder. "So what did you do? As a Faerie I mean."

"My father is a bond guard to the queen, Aoife. My mother is her sister and a teacher. I was a, *am* a law giver."

"Aoife is your aunt? You're a deity of justice? A warrior?"

"Yes, she's my aunt, and I'm not a deity. That's a human word with human understanding. I'm not a god, I'm just a Faerie and my job is almost like what human judges do. An

37

interpreter of laws, not a warrior although my ego would be less bruised if you hadn't asked with such disbelief in your voice." His voice was dry and she snickered.

"Stop it. Jeez, the ego on you. You're hotter than hot and I like brains on a man. You said you're royalty?"

Mollified, he relaxed back into the seat. "Minor royalty but yes. A prince."

"Oh, just a prince." She snorted and he hid a smile.

"Why haven't you been here in a while? You mentioned last night that you'd needed to visit but hadn't." He wanted to know her, wanted to understand her.

"I love my grandmother very much. Spent summers and the winter holidays here growing up. My grandmother was always different from my parents. I told you they're scientists. She's...well she's magic. I suppose you know that given the wards at my flat."

She was silent for some minutes and he let her be.

"I grew up with this dichotomy in my universe. Magic was real but my parents, my mother especially, were not behind that. Ration was king in my house. I grew up reading Kant and the other masters of reason. History and language became my great loves despite this part of myself that's a mystery. A part that scares me although admittedly I'm curious about it.

"I came to see her six months ago and we got into an argument. She told me my parents had been hiding something from me and she wanted me to know. I've been in the middle my whole life and I resent it."

"I can understand why you'd be uncomfortable," he said.

Hitting the steering wheel with the heel of her hand, she let out an explosive sigh. "It's more than that. I think I knew even then she was telling the truth and I couldn't face it. Facing it would have meant I had to confront that my parents had lied about something very important and I wasn't ready so I let this be about my gran but it's really about me. And damn if I don't really hate it when I have to be all self-reflective and stuff."

He grinned, admiring her ability to be honest about her motivations. "It looks good on you, Irish witch. I'm sure she'll understand."

"She'll poke at me with it a bit and let it go. I have to brace myself for whatever it is."

He realized that was probably what scared her most and resolved to be as supportive as he could through it. Whatever it was. So much on their plate. She amazed him that she hadn't broken down with all the stuff she had to process.

"I have more questions for you, most notably about this crazy bitch who cursed you but we're here. I'll let my gran take over with the questioning," she said as they turned down a long drive toward a whitewashed house at the end of the lane.

When Haley pulled the car to a stop, a wolfhound came to greet them. Haley bent, speaking softly to him, scratching behind his ears. "Hello, Elvis. Is my grandmother around?"

"She's right here. And you didn't tell me you'd mated with a Faerie."

Startled, Conall looked up and saw a woman walking toward them, holding a basket filled with fresh laundry. She stopped, looking him up and down, thrust the basket at him and turned to Haley. "Sweetness, it's about time you've come around to see me. Over your silly tantrum finally?"

"I'm sorry, Gran. I am. It was stupid to run out and I didn't mean all that stuff I said about you trying to go around Mom and Dad." Haley looked so small as her grandmother pulled her into a hug. Longing hit Conall hard, he couldn't wait to see his own mother again.

"Come in. I know you didn't mean it." She drew Haley toward the back steps and tossed a look back at Conall over her shoulder. "You too, handsome. There's a long story to be told, I'd wager."

Once inside, Haley's grandmother turned on the water for tea and Haley helped, measuring out the leaves and placing biscuits on a pretty plate.

"Gran, this is Conall Shaunessey or rather macCormac. Conall, this is my grandmother, Maeve O'Brian."

Conall bowed over her hand, kissing it. "It is my pleasure to meet Haley's grandmother. She speaks very highly of you."

"Of course she does. I'm her gran and she was raised right, even if her father is afraid of his heritage and her gifts. Now, come on through. I need to fold this and you need to tell me how a *Daoine Sidhe* came to be standing in my kitchen, mated to my granddaughter. While you're at it, you can tell me why you stink of a curse."

Haley was right about Maeve O'Brian. Formidable was a weak word for this woman. He liked her, saw where Haley got her grit.

He followed Maeve into the front room and Haley brought up the rear with a tray carrying the tea and biscuits.

Haley helped her grandmother fold laundry while Conall told the basic story of the curse and how Haley had broken it and created their bond.

"Hmpf." Maeve sat down and Haley poured her a cup of tea, placing it in front of her.

"I'm going to take your laundry up to your room. I don't like you walking up and down the stairs with that basket."

Maeve looked at Haley and rolled her eyes. With a flick of her wrist the basket disappeared. "I don't carry it up and down the stairs. Now sit down. Conall is going to tell me how he plans to deal with the one who cursed him."

A cold chill slid down his spine where it'd been building since Haley mentioned it in the car. How could he have neglected to think of that? Ninane, if she were still alive, would hear when he returned. Haley would be in danger until his tribe took her in as one of their own. Panic choked him for a moment but Maeve's voice broke through and he suspected she'd put a bit of magic in it to calm him.

"I see you hadn't thought of that."

Haley looked between them, confused. "I brought it up in the car. But you'll both have to explain carefully here. I feel like you're speaking a foreign language."

"The one who cursed him, if she's still alive, will still want to harm him and because you're his, you as well. Do I have the right of it?" Maeve looked to him with clear, green eyes.

He nodded with a sigh. "Mrs. O'Brian, if you don't mind, what are you? I can sense your magic, see it's Faerie in origin. What are you doing living out here instead of with your people?"

"Ah, that. Well, yes. My parents were Traveling Folk. My first husband was of my tribe. My mate. I loved him with my entire being. We had three thousand years together. He was killed along with all my sons but one, Haley's father. You see, a noble from below had taken a special shine to me and resented Bruch, that was my husband, and my family. He felt if he had them removed, I'd go to him. I killed him instead and ran. I settled here with my son, and I met a human, a mage of sorts and practitioner of the white arts. I felt as much love for him as I could, but it was a shadow of what I'd had. Cian, Haley's dad, grew up and forgot his life under the hill. He wanted to, and I let him because it was less painful.

"But when Haley came, I remembered the joy of new life

41

and I tried very hard to convince Cian and Mary to move back here, but he refused. He wanted his child to grow up with ration and reason, not having her believe in the unseen and lights in the meadow at midnight. I argued enough to get him to agree to let me have her every summer for a month and they did come at Yule every year. But we had an agreement that until she reached twenty-five, I couldn't tell her about her origins."

Haley's eyes were wide as she stared at her grandmother. "*Cian?*"

"He changed his name to Joseph when he went to university." Maeve shrugged. "He was grown, I couldn't stop him."

"He's aging. How can he be aging if you're what? How old are you?" Haley pushed out of her chair and began to pace.

"I'm nearing five thousand human years old. Your father is round about three hundred but he's aging like a human. But now he's got a human lifespan and he's about sixty human years old. I'm sorry, Haley. I wanted you to know all this as you grew up but I made a promise. A vow. And part of the vow was because your father gave up his immortality to confer it to you. He's given you his power and his magic. Each year he forgets more and more of what he was. In another decade, he won't remember the shining folk who used to visit us when he was small."

She blinked and swayed for a moment and Conall reached out to steady her, aching for her.

"Why? Why would he do that? He's going to die and for what? Why did no one ask me if that's what I wanted?"

"Darling girl, your father is very much like his own father, your grandfather. Stubborn, strong, courageous. He had something that would protect you and he loves you more than anything. He rejected his identity a long time ago so he gave it to you, and when he did that, he gave you the most precious thing he had other than his love. And he loves your mother. She's human. He didn't want to live as she got old and died."

"She has a hint of Fae but doesn't feel full blooded. Why?" As much as he worried for Haley's feelings, Conall had to admit he felt a lot better knowing she had the gifts of a full-blooded Fae. She'd have his lifespan, the problems they faced would be a hell of lot less daunting now.

Maeve looked at her granddaughter. "I have to perform the last part of the spell. That's what I tried to speak with her about when she was here last and ran off. Conferring it all on her earlier would have been too much for her to bear, it might have broken her. But she's strong enough now. And without her full knowledge of what she was, she'd have been a target. Not knowing has protected her, just as a masking spell has dampened most of her power."

Maeve stood and went to the highboy near the doorway. She pulled out a bottle and three glasses, pouring the whiskey into them. Handing one to Haley and then Conall, she stood in front of her granddaughter. "I love you. I wish I could have been a bigger part of your life. Your parents love you, they did what they thought was best, including your father. This royal Fae behind you loves you. I know you're reeling from all this. A lesser woman would be weeping right about now. But you're not a lesser woman. You're of my line, an old and noble line of queens. You are Fae and nothing you do can change that. It's a gift. Your magic is a gift. The way you can intuit languages and symbols is a gift. Embrace it and embrace who and what you are. And while you're at it, embrace what your father has chosen for himself. Lady knows I don't understand it, but I respect it."

Haley drank the smoky amber liquid in three swallows and put the glass down before hugging her grandmother. "I don't know what to think, Gran. This is all so much! Yesterday morning I just wanted a jerk on my staff to obey international law and now I've got a Faerie boyfriend and I'm one too? There's a crazy Faerie who may still be alive and want to harm Conall still? My father gave up his life for me without asking and then hid it from me? I'm..." she shook her head, "...I'm stunned. What does all this mean? What the heck am I supposed to do?"

Conall snorted. Boyfriend. He was a hell of a lot more than that.

Maeve held Haley at arm's length. "It means you have a complicated life all the sudden, Haley. You've grown up in one world but your life is about to change in a big way. You've done the human thing. You've had a life made of rules and theories and that's been a huge comfort but there's always been a part of you that knew there was more. And now you'll see it with new eyes.

"Haley, you're Fae and once I complete the spell, you'll feel the true rush of your power. All you can do is be who you are. And that hasn't changed. You'll have new magic, more powerful magic, gifts you may not even suspect you had. A whole new part of your life is about to begin. So many wonderful and beautiful things are about to happen to you and I'm so excited for you. I know you'll be apprehensive, this is all totally new and you'll be off balance in Conall's world. But it'll be your world soon enough and you'll be immortal. A lot, I know. But who you are in here," she tapped Haley's temple, "and in here," she tapped Haley's chest over her heart, "will be the same tomorrow."

"I'll help you through in whatever way I can, you know." Conall wanted to go to her, to comfort her but he had to take solace in speaking from his place on the couch. Clearly Maeve needed to work things through with her granddaughter.

Haley turned to him, touched and still unsteady. "Thanks. I'm going need all the help I can get."

"Shall I complete the spell? Are you ready for that?" Her gran was all business after that little speech. Who knew her grandmother understood her so well? She was scared, not just scared but freaked. Everything in her life had been set, governed by what she could see and prove and suddenly, um, not so much. But her grandmother also knew exactly how hard to push and the switch to a more dispassionate way of dealing with things was just what Haley needed right then. If she'd been really emotional, Haley might have lost it.

Haley sighed and dealt with it the best she could. No hiding from it, it was suddenly her life and nothing was going to change that. "Ready? How the heck do I know? But I trust you, Gran. Do your thing."

Maeve nodded and looked over Haley's shoulder at Conall. "And then you're going to tell me what you're planning to do about the shebitch who cursed you and how you'll keep my girl safe."

He definitely had some planning to do. The last thing he wanted was to put Haley in harm's way. He'd go home and seek his family out and work with them to keep her safe. If he was lucky, Ninane would already be dead or punished in some way.

"Sit, I'll be right back." Maeve gestured absently as she left the room.

Haley turned and saw Conall on the couch looking better than any man had a right to. The long hair really did it for her. He looked downright edible.

"What are you thinking, Irish witch?" He patted the couch next to him and she moved there, allowing him to snuggle her into his side.

"I'll tell you later. Oh man, this week is going to turn my

45

hair gray."

"Haley, you're going to be immortal and full-blooded Fae. This makes you safer and relieves me of the pain of watching you get old and die as I stay young. You can be at my side, in my bed, forever. That's not something to make you gray, is it?"

She smiled. "I've known you for six months. I've had my share of fantasies about you, I certainly like you but this whole mystical soul mate thing? Kinda odd. And now the truth that my father gave up immortality and conferred it on me? And he's forgetting who he was? I don't know what to think."

"After you meet my family, we'll go away. Somewhere sunny and tropical. I'll feed you grapes and rub suntan lotion on your breasts," he murmured into her ear and her body tightened. God he was good at that.

"Okay, ready?" Her gran entered the room with a small box.

"Um, as I'll ever be."

"Roll that rug up, Conall, please."

Conall got up and rolled the large area rug in the room, exposing a magical circle etched into the hardwood below. Haley had first learned rudimentary magic in that circle.

"Well, that's handy then." Conall nodded with approval.

"Indeed. The floors are oak for strength with rowan for protection." Gran turned to Haley. "Take the box. Once inside the circle, open it and break the vial within. Don't open the circle until I say."

Haley took a deep breath and her gran handed her the box, which felt strangely heavy for such a small thing. Gran kissed her forehead and Conall her lips.

Centering herself and grounding her magic, Haley stepped into the circle and spoke the words to seal it behind her, felt the flare of the protection it gave her.

She unhooked the small catch on the lid and opened it. A heart-shaped vial lay inside, filled with what appeared to be pale green and blue smoke. Haley put the box on the floor and stood again, the glass heart warm in her hands.

"Here I go." She snapped the heart in half and the colored smoke drifted out and began to swirl around her, closer and closer until it rested against her like a second skin when it suddenly inverted and she felt it just inside her body.

Nothing for long seconds until tremors began to build in her muscles and electric waves of power roiled through her, filling her until it felt like she'd burst. Her back arched and she fell to her knees as it rode her. She gnashed her teeth, trying to hold onto the scream that wanted to free itself and when it did, she knew she spoke a language she hadn't known ten minutes prior.

When she opened her eyes, the world was beautiful. Her father had given this up for her and she swore to herself to never take for granted the gift he'd bestowed upon her. The home she'd spent her summers in wasn't just a comfortable place with tinges of magic, the magic here sang. Smudges of brilliant color painted the air and when she looked at Conall, she saw him as a prince. His aura shined bright blue and white and her heart beat in time with his. Never in her life had she been more sure of anything than she was right then. They were made for one another. It wasn't metaphysical romance novel hype, it was simply magical and she was blessed to have it.

He stood anxiously at her gran's side, holding her hand tight, worry clear on his face. When Haley smiled and stood up shakily, he heaved a sigh of relief.

"Break the circle then, Haley, and step out. Embrace your life as you embark on a new path." Her grandmother was so beautiful to Haley's new vision, it nearly hurt to look at her.

Haley said the words to break the circle and stepped out. Invisible threads tied her to Conall and pulled her to him. She felt that acutely but not in a bad way. It was comforting, reassuring. But her need to touch him rode her until he took her hand and kissed her fingertips.

"Um, wow."

Gran laughed and kissed both cheeks. "It worked, I see. Welcome. How do you feel?"

"Everything is so vivid, full of life and energy. Colors everywhere. I've only had this sort of experience when I used my inner sight. Never this sharp. Is this how you both see every day?"

"It's a gift to see the true beauty of the universe is it not? And why we love nature and animals so much. Everything is alive with energy. That energy is sacred in some sense, even negative energy." Gran looked to Conall. "I expect you'll be taking her to your *brugh*?"

He nodded. "I'll be wanting her to meet my family, be given the protection of my tribe. I'd like to extend my invitation to you as well."

Gran shook her head. "Thank you, but no. My place isn't with the shining folk just now. It's here with my house and my animals. I do visit my tribe several times a year. But Haley needs to be embraced by her new folk to learn and to be kept safe by their magic. I'll be wanting to be kept apprised of the situation now so don't go off without letting an old woman hear updates."

"Are you sure, Gran? Aren't you lonely for your family?"

"You're sweet to worry. But I have my own path. My sister, your great-aunt, comes to visit monthly. Your great-grandmother is still with us and she'll be wanting to finally meet you. You'll have a place with them as well. But for now, take this step. You have all the time in the world now. Go on, I expect your man will be anxious to see his own again."

"Can we leave the vehicle here?" Conall asked. They didn't need to drive to the *sithein*.

"Of course. Before you go, Haley, I want you to have these." Gran handed Haley a velvet pouch. Inside was a necklace and an armband decorated with horses. "They're marks of rank. Wear them with pride."

Conall's eyes widened as he took them in and his gaze moved back to Gran. "Madam, you didn't say you were royalty as well." He bowed.

Gran laughed, waving it away. "Ah well, you know how it is, Conall. Most of us are royalty in some way or other."

"It's more than that. You're descended from Macha."

Shock rang through Haley. "Wow, well no wonder I've always loved horses."

"Riding is a handy skill. You've always had the touch with animals. She would be proud of you. *Is* I'm sure on whatever plane she exists on now. I haven't seen her since I was small. Will you allow me to dress you in something more appropriate to meet your new family?"

"Um, sure. I guess jeans aren't really formal enough."

Gran tutted and with a flick of a wrist, Haley was suddenly outfitted in a long gown of deepest green. Golden ribbon bound her waist and between her breasts, all with horses woven into it. The armband gleamed and the necklace hung warm against her chest.

"You look so beautiful." Conall looked her up and down and kissed her nose. "Your gran isn't saying but I'll tell you her tribe is a very old and respected one. My family will be honored to have you among us. Ah, and your ears." He reached out to trace the tip and she felt a tingle in her nipples as her clit throbbed.

She moved to a mirror and saw her hair had grown longer and her ears were now pointed. "Get out! I have elf ears! Gran, how come you don't?"

Her gran laughed. "I do, darling. I wear a glamour when you're here." She tucked her hair back to show Haley.

"I am going to have a long talk with my parents. I can't believe they kept me from my heritage all this time." The more she thought about it, the more it hurt.

Gran shook her head and took Haley's face between her palms. "Sweetie, you'll have to let go of the anger. They did it out of a misguided need to protect you. And now your dad doesn't even remember half of it. Embrace your future and let go of the mistakes in the past. No good can come of it."

Haley took a deep breath and calmed down. "We'll see." But a part of her whispered that they kept it from her because they were ashamed of what she was. Would they feel differently about her now? She shook her head, her gran was right that there wasn't any good in letting thoughts like that affect her. "Will you be all right here?"

Her gran laughed. "Darling, I'm a tough old woman. Go on with you. You're going to be amazed by what you see." She turned to Conall and kissed his cheeks. "Keep her well or you'll have me to contend with."

He grinned. "Of course, my lady." Conall held his arm to Haley. "Shall we go then?"

"No time like the present."

She took his arm and suddenly they stood in a field in front of a small hill. She felt the magic there very strongly, the thick currents swirling around her.

"Home," he said quietly and approached the hillside. He

spoke under his breath and she had no complaints when he stood wearing a kilt and a sleeveless shirt, the markings on his shoulder blazing deep blue as a door appeared in the grass.

She blinked several times at the appearance of the door, a plain wooden door with an antiqued handle.

"Here we are." He paused, looking into her face. "Haley, before we go inside, do you feel it? The connection between us? Is it different now that you're full Fae?"

She nodded. "Like ribbons of magic connect us. I can see you, I mean really *see* you." Shrugging, she tried to describe it but there weren't words accurate enough. But right then, it was just about the only thing she was totally sure of. "It's right. I know that. I know we're meant to be and it feels like that's all I need to know."

Smiling, he bent and kissed her. "Yes, indeed. Well, come through then. See the world hidden to your eyes until now."

Chapter Four

He opened the door and a cool rush of magic met them. Beyond the door wasn't a dark cave but a bright garden filled with flowers and trees. Haley held on to Conall's hand as he led her through and her life shifted yet again.

When she looked over her shoulder, the door was gone and all that remained was a hillside just like the one she'd stood at before they entered. Weird!

Her heart constricted at the look on his face. Wonder and pain. How he must have hated his life, so devoid of color and emotion for so long. Knowing *this* existed and he had no way to get to it.

All at once, she felt totally in over her head. Well, more over her head than she'd felt before. He had this life—this life he'd lived for centuries before she even existed and he'd been estranged from it for so long. She had no connection to it, no real understanding of it other than looking into his face and seeing his pain. She'd only known him for six months. How could she begin to be supportive? A small part of her worried he'd find her wanting when he compared her to his old life.

Despite her insecurities, he deserved to have his life back. The last thing she wanted was to make him feel bad or to take his focus from his family. The moment was all about him and he didn't need to take care of her. She squeezed his hand and he turned to her, smiling with unshed tears in his eyes.

"It's beautiful." She wanted him to know she thought it was special. And in truth, she wanted to know this world with him. It was her world now as well, part of her identity. She wished it wasn't so scary letting go of the old and having such a giant pool of new to jump into.

Relieved, she saw the sadness in his eyes ease a bit as he smiled at her. "This is just the beginning. Come on, through the gates there ahead. There'll be sentries and we can alert my family."

His long legs ate up the last few feet leading to large gates where guards stood beyond.

"Is that wood?" She examined the material the gates were crafted from.

"Sort of. The myth about cold iron is actually true. The wood is enchanted. It's unbreakable..." He trailed off as he caught sight of the sentries just beyond the gates. When he called out, one turned and looked at him, and looked again, frozen to the spot.

"It can't be..."

"It is. Mal, come on and let me in. Me and Haley, my wife. Send someone ahead to tell my family I'm here and alive." Haley heard the emotion in Conall's voice and it sliced her open.

The one Conall called Mal walked toward the gate slowly, opening it and standing aside. "Lady, it's you!" He turned to the other sentry. "Go and alert Dana and Cormac!" The sentry ran off and Mal turned back to them. "Come in, come in and bring your...did you say wife? Well," he winked in Haley's direction, "she's pretty but she must have vision problems if she let you catch her."

As she passed through the gates, the magic of the wards on the other side rippled around her, admitted her and embraced her. She watched as the sentry pulled Conall into a hug. They lapsed into what should have been a foreign language, she knew it was, and yet she understood it.

"Dev has gone to alert your mother. Let's walk while you tell me what happened. Lady knows there'll be a high fuss when everyone begins to hear and rush to the square. But you've failed to introduce me to this lovely redhead you've obviously enchanted." He bent at the waist to Haley, making her blush.

Conall laughed. "I...she's...yes, this is my heart." He looked down at Haley with such love, such depth of emotion toward her she felt it to her toes. A rush of longing, of desire, comfort, love, fear, anxiety and joy swamped her all at once. She felt a little dizzy for a moment but it passed.

"Malcolm macDonal, this is my wife, Haley. Haley, this is one of my oldest friends, Malcolm."

Haley held out a hand and Malcolm took it, kissing her knuckles. "Traveling Folk are always welcome within these gates."

As they walked, they entered into a sort of town square and a chorus of voices got louder and louder until a group of people burst into the open space and the woman at the head of the group halted, her hand over her mouth to stifle a cry.

"*Máthair...*" Conall moved toward the woman slowly at first until she opened her arms and he rushed into them.

Tears blurred Haley's vision as she watched Conall and his mother embrace. She lost sight of him for long minutes as more and more Fae came and joined the throng. A bone-deep weariness settled over her. The day suddenly felt very long. Guilt settled as she pushed past it. This was his moment, his day and she didn't want him to worry about anything but seeing his family again.

A bright-haired woman who looked to be Haley's age

approached her. "And who are you, then? You've got the markings of the Traveling Folk. You're clearly one of Macha's. I'm Rhona, one of Conall's cousins."

"That's my wife." Conall jogged up to them, pulling her to his side with a wide grin. She felt the joy radiate from him and a small slice of sadness at what her father had done without her knowing edged through her as well.

"Um, wife?" she mumbled. He kept referring to her that way and she knew they had some mystical hoodoo thing between them but a quick boink, *several* boinks and they were married? Wasn't there a ceremony or something?

But no one heard her because at his announcement, the throng moved to them, excitedly chattering and hugging her.

"Back up a bit! That's my daughter-in-law and I haven't been able to clap eyes on her yet. And there's still the matter of my son explaining why he's been thought of as dead for a thousand years."

Haley looked up into the face of the woman who so obviously gave birth to Conall. Hair dark as a raven's wing, eyes as blue as her son's. The same regal features only a bit softer.

"I'm Dana, please be welcome here." Smiling, she kissed Haley's cheeks and took her hands. "Come, let's go to the house. We'll have a meal and Conall can tell us the whys of this."

Conall pushed a lock of Haley's hair behind her ear before moving his attention back to his mother. "We need to extend the protection of our tribe to Haley immediately and block any access to Ninane. She is the cause of my disappearance."

Gasps filled the square.

"She left us nearly eight hundred years past. Where there is trouble, her fingers can likely be found. Has she threatened Haley?"

Before Conall could answer his mother, one of the biggest men Haley had ever seen muscled his way into the square. He stopped as he caught sight of them and Conall blinked slowly.

"Son! They said you'd returned but I didn't believe them." Warrior braids swinging, the man lumbered to Conall and hugged him, kissing the top of his head as if Conall were a mere toddler.

"Da, you're well?" Conall asked when his father released him and the noise began anew when Conall introduced him to Haley.

Haley felt as if she couldn't draw enough breath. So many people looking at her, asking her questions, touching her. She was a lifetime away from everything she'd ever known. Everything she didn't have now that she'd become immortal. Consciousness sucked at her as her vision narrowed. She clutched Conall's arm for balance before she fell over.

"Haley? You're so pale. Irish witch, are you all right?" Conall asked urgently.

"I don't think so. I need some air. I'm sorry." Weakness settled in and she wondered what the hell was going on.

Dana tsked loudly and shoved her way through the crowd with one hand. "Bring that girl to the house, Conall. Can't you see how overwhelmed she is? Cormac, come on then! Have someone tell my sister Conall has returned and we need her for a ceremony at the house immediately."

Haley saw the royalty in the way her mother-in-law expected to be obeyed without question, even as she was relieved when Conall picked her up and carried her, his face drawn with concern.

"We can't sift in here. Within the boundaries of the gates, that sort of magic is prohibited. My parents' house is ahead," he explained to her as they walked.

56

"Sift?" she asked faintly, the pretty lane beginning to spin.

"It's a manner of moving from place to place. Darlin'?" Conall spoke with his lips against her temple. "Are you ill?"

She shook her head. "No. I'm...sort of dizzy and feeling very weak all the sudden. I suppose it was because there were so many people and...I'm so embarrassed!"

"There's nothing to be embarrassed about. Just rest your head on my shoulder. We're almost there."

His heart beating against her ear on his chest reassured her as she watched the scenery pass by through half-lidded eyes.

The house they approached was lovely, sandy white with a carpet of purple-blue flowers all around the walk. Big windows and a large door decorated the front looking over the hillside that sloped down to the square they'd just been in.

"Bring her inside, Conall. Let's get her lying down and some food into her. She's pale." Conall's father opened the door and ushered them inside as a squealing group ran up behind them and nearly knocked Conall over while he held Haley still in his arms.

"You'll be wanting to calm down now! Your brother is holding his wife and he won't want to drop her. She's feeling a bit poorly." Conall's mother shook her head at the group of women who stepped back, each talking all at once.

"Put her down here, son." The big man smiled down at Haley after Conall put her on a soft couch. Conall had some of the other man's features but his hair was a bit lighter, nose broader. It was plain he was a warrior though his eyes took her in kindly and he spoke gently. "I'm Cormac, Conall's da. It's very nice to meet you, sweet girl. I always loved a woman with red hair." He winked and Haley saw where Conall got his charm.

57

Cormac took her hand, pressing it between both of his briefly.

"Here, drink this." Dana moved Cormac aside and handed Haley a glass of sweet-smelling liquid. "It's juice. It should perk you up. Have you eaten today?"

"Please, please don't worry about me. Conall, visit with your family. They'll have missed you so much. I'm sorry to have made a scene." Haley was mortified over the whole thing.

Her new mother-in-law shook her head and urged Haley to keep drinking. "Be quiet about that, you. Easily three hundred Fae filled that square all talking at once. Pushing and shoving to see Conall again after we'd thought him dead. Anyone would have been overwhelmed." Dana smiled and Haley relaxed as she sat up and drank the juice.

Conall moved her over a bit and sat next to her. He encircled her gently with one arm, his fingers tracing up and down her side. Immediately she felt better at his touch.

He'd begun to tell his family the story when Aoife entered the house. Haley knew it had to be the Fae queen because the power she brought with her was an unmistakable tide. She had the ebony hair her sister and nephew bore but hers trailed the back of her calves. Eyes an otherworldly amethyst complimented pale and luminous skin. She might have been petite compared to the other Fae Haley had seen but there was nothing fragile about her at all. Aoife's magic throbbed from her body.

Conall lifted his head and caught sight of his aunt. Gently, he moved from Haley's side and fell to his knees. With a sob, Aoife knelt, hugging him. Soon everyone was crying and hugging and Haley watched as the whole scene unfolded, tears in her own eyes.

"Tell me, Conall. Why have you been gone so long? What

happened?" Aoife stood and Conall returned to Haley's side. It was then Aoife noticed Haley and one regal eyebrow rose as she smiled. "And who is this lovely young thing?"

"That's his bride, Haley. Let him finish the story and we'll do introductions. She needs to rest just now." Dana patted Haley's shoulder as she explained to her sister.

Aoife obviously knew what it was to be ordered around by her sister because she snorted and winked at Haley before sitting across from them. "Go on then."

Conall told them the rest of the story and Aoife's face drew into a concerned, angry mask. Cormac swore darkly and various family members began to mutter and move about agitatedly. The magic in the room swirled about Haley, marked by anger and pain as well as joy and relief. She'd never been exposed to so many people with magic before.

Despite still feeling totally overwhelmed, she managed to hang on. She didn't want to interrupt any more of the reunion.

"Dear Lady. This is insanity." Cormac began to pace, fingering the lethal sword he wore at his side.

Aoife simply shook her head. "She will be taken care of. No one can be allowed to get away with harming my family or members of my tribe. Now, let's meet this lovely redhead of yours." Her look of anger dissolved as she focused on Haley.

Conall stood and turned to Haley, holding his hand out. She managed to stand without swaying and without really knowing what the heck to do, she curtseyed to Aoife.

"Aunt, this is my wife Haley. Haley, my aunt Aoife, Queen of the *Daoine Sidhe*." Conall braced her weight with his arm around Haley's waist. Her magic surged and then settled again.

Aoife touched the top of Haley's head. "No need to bow to me. Be welcome to our *sithein* and our tribe. Its protections are yours as you are ours."

Haley's spine straightened as the magic shot through her. Apparently Aoife had just given the protection of the tribe to her. Or something, because a heck of a lot of magic barreled through her system.

"Yes, that was me extending the protection of this place, of our people to you, Haley. Thank you for bringing Conall back to us. Your skill and magic will be most welcome here. You look like your grandmother. How is Maeve?"

Lawd, did the queen read minds too? "She's well, thank you. I didn't know you knew her." She was going to have a long talk with her gran about what was a *fun* surprise and what was just a surprise.

"Conall, the girl is about to fall over. What's going on?" Dana moved forward and put her hand on Haley's forehead. For a moment, Haley thought it was amusing the gesture was in common across species lines.

"Haley, are you sick? What is it? This is more than simply being overwhelmed by the number of people out there earlier." Conall sat her back down, looking at her concernedly.

"I feel faint. I'm sure it's just being tired. I felt so good after that spell my gran performed earlier. Probably haven't eaten enough today."

"Spell?" Aoife asked.

Conall explained to them about the way Haley's father had conferred his immortality and full magic and power on her and how her grandmother had performed the spell to render her fully Fae that morning.

"Why didn't you say so? Conall, that kind of spell would have pushed a great deal of magic into her when she wasn't used to it. Haley was half-Fae with a small bit of magic until a few hours ago. Suddenly, the magic of an immortal and all that comes with it was thrust into her. That's quite a bit of energy to absorb. She'd have been very energized at first but as her magic entered the *brugh* and she interacted with all of us her system would have to work very hard to equalize. It's a wonder she's even conscious." Aoife spoke to Conall and Haley would have been annoyed they hadn't addressed her but she couldn't seem to keep her eyes open.

"I could have killed her with my stupidity?"

Haley's anger surged enough to bring her back to consciousness. "Hey! Don't blame yourself. This is something new for me too. I'm not dead. In fact, I'm immortal. So cut the guilt." She slumped back against the couch and heard Cormac chuckle.

"The girl is a lot like her mother-in-law. Conall, boyo, you're in for it. I like her. Your house is still kept up. Your sisters have gone by now and again and freshened the place. Your mother and I have made sure the wards haven't died. It just felt like a way to...well, a way to keep you alive." Cormac blushed a bit and Conall reached out to squeeze his father's hand.

"Your father never believed you dead," Dana said softly. "There'll be time for this enough later. Get the girl into bed. She'll be fine after some rest. I'll send Aideen over with some tea and herbs to burn while she's resting."

"Thank you. We'll come by later." Conall picked her up again and she felt the magic of those in the room surround her and slide into her system to help. It was as if they gave her a hug with their energy and it made her want to cry. It made her miss her own mother.

Aoife pressed a kiss to Haley's cheek. "We're your family now too, *pis chumhra*. Rest."

The queen of the Fae had just called her sweet pea. How cool was that?

"We'll plan a party. A welcome home and wedding party.

61

We'll avenge your loss, Conall. *Our* loss. She tore our child from us, stole the conscience of this place and it cannot stand." Cormac kissed his son's cheek and Haley sighed happily before falling into unconsciousness.

Chapter Five

Conall looked out the windows of his study, past the wall of his books. His muscles trembled, still twitching as he stared out over the wildflower-covered slope leading to the glistening lake below.

Nearly a thousand years without emotion had caught up to him and he'd only barely put Haley's sleeping body down in his—their—bed before he'd begun to drown.

Setting a ward to alert him if she stirred or called out, he'd headed down to his study, a place where he'd always felt comforted and safe in the past. His knees buckled and he'd begun to weep in deep, gut-wrenching sobs.

So much had been stolen from him. His family had moved forward. He had four siblings. The sister just younger than he was had mated and married and had children. They lived in another *sithein* and he'd need to take Haley to meet them sometime soon. The sister just younger than her, Brenna, had married and had children as well. The baby of the family, Aideen, hadn't yet taken a husband but lived in the *brugh*. Lastly, Conall's older brother Riordan had spent generations learning how to be a warrior and teaching it to the Fae here within the *brugh*. Conall was disappointed to hear his brother was off on a top secret mission of some sort and wouldn't be back for another few weeks.

Overall, not a whole lot had changed about how the *brugh* looked, with the exception of another pub. His world had continued on without him as he'd lived, wrapped in the cotton of his emotionless state, lifetime after lifetime.

After the tears, the rage had come. He'd broken a few things, pulled books from the shelves on the far side of the room, overturned furniture as he'd fumed. That bitch had stolen his life! She'd scared his family and made them think him dead or lost to them.

And now, hours later, he'd reached an equilibrium of sorts as it all eased and he felt love. Love for his family, his tribe and the woman in their bed. Without the curse, he'd never have met Haley and for that reason, he could actually thank Ninane for her treachery. After he killed her perhaps.

An ever-present anxiety blanketed his feelings. Ninane continued to haunt his thoughts. She posed a threat. A bigger one than he'd let on to Haley. Ninane was powerful and even nine hundred years ago had bordered on insane. Once she found out he was back he'd bet everything he had, she'd be back to her old tricks.

But the problem was, he had more to lose than his life or his soul. He had Haley and any fool could see using Haley was the easiest way to get to Conall.

He itched to rush out and find Ninane right then. To kill her and end the threat before it touched Haley. Breathing out, he tried to manage all the emotions he'd been without for so long. He needed to get himself in check, to remember how to deal with feeling anything at all.

Hunger hit him and he realized he needed to check on Haley as well. She had to be hungry too. He needed to be sure she took care of herself. He wasn't the only one dealing with a rush of new experiences. Seeing her so pale and weak had done something to him. After centuries without emotion, the intensity of what he felt for his woman nearly felled him.

He'd loved before, back before the curse. Fae put a lot of stock in family and love. But all the women in the past couldn't stand up to what he felt for Haley.

As he'd grown up and still lived with his parents, he remembered catching the two of them looking at each other, or touching each other. Just a glance or a caress and so much passed between them it was as if no one else existed. He hadn't understood it even as he'd grown past embarrassment and into a sort of yearning to have that kind of connection.

And totally out of the blue, Haley O'Brian had walked into his office and set his world upside down. She'd given him back his soul. He didn't have any fear that he only loved her because of the magic of the bond. She was meant for him. Period. To question that would be silly.

As if he'd called to her, the wards flared and he heard her moving about in the bedroom at the top of the stairs. He moved toward her, needing to know she was all right.

She stood at the head of the stairs, hair tousled and looking much better. A smile curved her lips.

He pulled her against his chest, breathing her in as her arms slid around his waist. "How are you feeling, darlin'?"

"Much better. How long was I out?"

He maneuvered her back toward the bedroom. "Several hours. I lost track of the exact time. Get back in bed. I'll magic us some food and we can eat under the blankets."

"Won't your family want to see you?" She let him push her back onto the bed and swung her legs beneath the covers. The bare flash of her creamy skin shot straight to his cock. Another thing about the bond between them was his need to touch her, take her scent into his lungs. Taste her.

He kissed her neck and she arched into his touch. He took a taste, the barest flick of his tongue to drag over her steady pulse. She was ill, he had to stop before the roar of his hormones and his need for her drowned out his concern.

"No. No. Don't stop. Please." Her voice was soft but he heard a need that mirrored his own. Her fingers dug into his shoulders, holding him to her.

"Haley, you've been ill. You need to rest." Even as he said it, the edge of his teeth scraped over her collarbone and she shivered.

"I need you. When you touch me it's all better. I feel all right."

He broke away enough to look into her eyes, those big green eyes of hers that saw right through him from day one. The transformation made them brighter, a bit more otherworldly but still *his* Haley looked back at him. Yes, passion tinged them but she was clearly in charge of her faculties.

"I don't want to hurt you." It was so important that never happen.

She let go and his relief warred with disappointment. Until she grabbed the shirt she'd been wearing, one of his he'd changed her into when he brought her home, and ripped it open. The pinging sound of buttons hitting furniture and then the floor echoed just barely over his breath as he struggled to control himself.

A struggle he lost when her breasts were bared to his gaze. A struggle she knew he'd lose when she brought her hands up to cup herself. A smile, then the flash of teeth as she caught her bottom lip, charmed him.

"You're a siren, you know." He pulled his shirt over his head and quickly shed his pants, coming back to lie naked with her.

"Me? I'm the one who wasn't wearing panties when I woke up. I know I had them on when I went to sleep, Conall."

He laughed. "Well, I like to see you bare." He drew his fingertips down her belly and over the lips of her pussy.

"Mmm, well, I'm the first woman in what, a thousand years, who's given you the green light. I'm guessing you'd like anyone who did that at this point."

He shifted and flicked the tip of his tongue over each nipple. "It's more than that. I need you to know it's so much more than that."

"I...I think so. I...I can't think when you're doing that! And if you stop I'll have to kill you."

Her growl was sufficiently cute enough the edge fell from his frustration.

"I knew you were mine the first moment I laid eyes on you. Mine, Haley. You were born to be and I was born to belong to you. Our magic mingles together right now as it did then. In nine hundred years not once did a woman stir me. Until you. You walked into my office and you looked right into me and knew me. *I know you.*"

He shifted, moving downward. "Your taste is lodged in me. Your scent has taken over my brain. When I close my eyes, it's your face I see. My hands itch to touch you."

She watched him, wide-eyed as he pushed her thighs apart and licked along the crease at the top of each leg. A soft gasp escaped those lips and he smiled, their gazes meeting as the air began to vibrate with their desire.

Sliding his hands beneath her, he lifted her up, serving her body to himself as he began to devour. Her scent, the earthy tang of her body made his cock throb against the bed. Lady, he needed her.

She was so wet, her honey coated his tongue as he licked through the furls of her pussy and over the swollen bundle of her clit. Soft sounds of entreaty murmured from her lips.

So good. So fucking good. Her pussy was the best thing he'd ever tasted.

A moan vibrated from deep within her as her hands grasped his hair. Side to side, he brushed his lips over her pussy, over her clit, as if he could never get enough. And he knew he never would.

A low hum filled the room as the very air seemed to throb. He knew when she began to climax as her magic rose from her like heat from the pavement. It caught his own magic, sucking at him, pulling him under with her as he heard her whisper his name over and over.

When her muscles relaxed, he gently lowered her to the bed and moved to lay beside her.

He thought they'd enjoy a soft, quiet moment but he was wrong. She got up, swinging her leg over his body and settled herself astride him.

"So, um, wow. Orgasm as a Faerie? Rocks. Just sayin'."

He laughed. "Why didn't you say, *orgasm with Conall* instead of the Fae thing?"

"I had an orgasm with Conall before I was a Faerie. Okay, three. And while they were all *way* above average orgasms, like the kind you read about in smutty books, what you just did to me? My teeth are vibrating. My ears! Oh man, you didn't tell me about the whole ear as an erogenous zone thing."

All the while she chattered, she undulated her hips, driving her hot, slick pussy over his cock until he ground out, "Put my cock inside you and stop teasing me or there'll be hell to pay!"

"Mmm! While that sounds very intriguing, I can't find it in

me to test that now."

Rising up, she reached back and guided the head of his cock to her gate and sank down, taking him deep into herself. A deep, bone-shattering groan broke from his lips at the sensation of being surrounded by her body.

He looked up into her face, over the swells of her pert, beautiful breasts as her hair slid back and forth over her shoulders like sunset-colored silk.

"Lady, you're beautiful."

He touched lips that smiled only for him and felt grateful, so very grateful, she existed and was his.

The look in Conall's eyes seared her deep. Such love there. Adoration. Trust. Admiration. Joy. Fear too.

She felt it as well. How fortunate she was to have this. However it came about, whatever brought it to her she couldn't feel resentful or distrustful of it. It simply was and she wasn't going to question it.

She shared his love, his adoration, trust and admiration. And his fear. Fear that this bitch who harmed him would come back to hurt him again. Fear she'd lose the best thing she'd ever tasted. And what would her world be like without Conall now that his life had touched hers? Bleak.

"Haley? Are you all right?"

She focused on his face, saw his concern. Unable to speak she nodded but a tear fell anyway and he sat up and scooted back to lean against the headboard, staying seated within her.

"What is it? Am I hurting you?"

"No," she managed to whisper. "I don't want to lose you. She won't come back will she? Teach me how to fight her, Conall." She could bear a lot, but losing him seemed totally unimaginable and yet, the anticipation she'd felt in the glade where the ring stood just a few days before remained and she had a strong suspicion it had everything to do with Ninane.

He smiled and kissed her tears away. "Lady, you slay me. So precious to me, sweet, sweet Irish witch. Ninane may try to come back. I won't lie. But she doesn't have the element of surprise she had before. She won't succeed if she tries to harm me. And I'll kill her before I'd let her harm you."

She nodded. "Okay. I love you, Conall. I know it seems soon. Hell, it *is* soon, but I do."

He kissed her lips softly. "Me too. I love you too. Now, if you're not going to do your job, you can't be on top."

Haley undulated on him, rolling her hips as she raised one eyebrow in his direction.

His breath stuttered. "Where'd you learn that, Irish witch?"

She continued with the movement, slow and sure. "I took a belly dancing class. I've never tried it this way. Pity."

Leaning in, he nipped her bottom lip, making her yelp as she laughed. "You'd better not have!"

"Conall," she continued, breathless from laughing, "you may have been forcibly chaste for a thousand years but I'm not so stupid I don't know you got it on with loads of chicks before that."

Putting a hand to his chest he gasped theatrically. "Got it on? You wound me! Are you suggesting I was loose?"

"A man whore? A floozy, or is that moozy if it's a guy? Oh get that look off your face! I'm guessing you were a connoisseur of women rather than a moozy."

"If you didn't have such talented hips I'd be vexed." He totally blew it when he started to laugh, rolling over and landing on top of her body, continuing to stroke into her.

He felt so damned good Haley thought she might die from it. The heightened sensation her magic gave her now that she was Fae was incredible. Like having her skin turned on to ten on the dial. Everywhere they touched was like a brush of her clit. Every inch of his cock sent ripples of pleasure through her pussy. Stretching her even as he caressed her internally. He existed within her, not just with his cock, but with their connection to one another. He was all around her and inside her. She was awash with him, with desire. Love filled her to overflowing. To say sex with Conall was mind-blowing would be an understatement. In truth she wasn't sure there were words adequate to describe the feeling of his cock as it pressed in and then retreated.

Haley arched her back, needing more of him. She raised her knees, wrapped her calves around his waist and dug her fingers into his shoulders. His hair caressed her bare chest and neck, his scent settled things within her even as it excited her.

Her orgasm began to build again and she let go of one shoulder to slide a hand between them. He groaned in her ear. "Goddess it's sexy when you do that. Soon, Irish witch, soon I'm going to put you on the table and sit back and watch your fingers coated in your honey, playing over your clit."

Her breath caught in her throat when her middle finger reached her clit and pressed gently. She didn't need to move, he provided the friction as he fucked into her body.

"Your pretty pale skin will glow with pleasure and I'll take my cock out. Lightly stroke it because I'll want to concentrate on you, with those fingers sliding into your pussy. Your head will fall back, you'll catch your bottom lip between your teeth the way you do and you'll make soft, needy sounds." With each word, his voice became deeper and more strained. She knew he was close and she was too.

"Oh, yes!" she gasped as orgasm rushed through her, sucking her under as her body gave over to endorphins designed to make her feel as if she floated in desire. His body on top of hers anchored her, kept her from drifting away as he arched back, thrusting into her hard and deep, and came as well.

Long moments later, he let out a satisfied sigh and rolled to the side, holding her against him as they caught their breath.

"Now, my family will be here in about half an hour. There's to be a large meal and everyone will ooh and aaah over you."

Haley sat up with a gasp. "Why didn't you tell me? Conall, I have to get ready. Shower. I don't have any clothes here. Oh man."

He grabbed her and pulled her back to him, kissing the top of her head. "I tried but you jumped me. Minx. And I saved you from a trip to my parents'. You should be grateful. They'll all come over here because my mother won't hear of you going anywhere for a day or so. Now, we will shower together. No, don't get that look, you're still weak and I shouldn't have had sex with you just now but I don't want you to fall. I can wait a few hours to have you again." He winked and tumbled out of bed, helping her to stand.

Chapter Six

Ninane stalked through the corridors of the castle, on her way to see the king. Anger and fear coursed through her system. It wasn't very often she received such an urgent summons. Like she was nothing more than a lowly servant with little better to do than drop everything and scurry to his throne room.

She sniffed her indignance as the guards opened the large doors so she could enter. She'd left the light and brilliance of Aoife's court for the dim, dark glitter of Dugan's. Still, he'd taken her in when Aoife had finally exiled her and she had a certain powerbase here among the phantoms.

"Ah, Ninane. I have news for you. Sit and have a glass of wine. You'll need it." Dugan, the dark-haired king wore an amused smile and Ninane knew whatever he had to say would be at her expense. Bastard.

Faking nonchalance, she sat and took the goblet of wine passed her way by a servant. "Well, tell me, Dugan."

"Conall macCormac is back."

The goblet tumbled from nerveless fingers. "What? Where?"

"It's all over the above. Conall is not only back and soul restored but he's also bonded. Her name is Haley. By all accounts she's quite lovely and the *Daoine* have taken to her well." His arched brow told Ninane he knew of her feelings for

Lauren Dane

Conall.

She'd known this day would come at some point but with each passing year, she'd grown complacent. Now he was back and soul restored. Her heart raced as her body heated. She'd been unable to watch him or even to know his identity when he was human but now... Now he was returned, living, breathing.

"You're up to something, Ninane."

"I am not," she snapped. "Now they'll know how he was lost to them but as Aoife has already banished me, it's of no consequence. I suppose we'll be hearing from Aoife soon."

Dugan chuckled. "I already have. She demanded you be turned over to her for trial."

Ninane refused to let him rile her. He wouldn't turn her over. He liked to watch her squirm nearly as much as he liked her in his bed. And her magic aided his little underworld playground.

"You're no fun." He gave a pretty pout and she snorted. "Of course I replied that as a member of my court, you were protected and that I heralded the safe return of her nephew. I was _shocked_ to hear of your part in his disappearance but since you'd been here, you've been a very useful member of our society."

"Well, there is a certain amount of amusement in imagining how her face must have looked in the scrying bowl when you refused. Was she very angry?" Ninane got up and moved to Dugan's lap. She needed to plan and keep him out of her business. Sex was as easy a way with him as anything else and he was moderately good at it.

"Mmm, very. She threatened to send her guards for you and I reminded her that would be war and we've been getting along so well these last centuries." His fingers drew the hem of her gown up her legs slowly.

74

"And his wife? What of her?" Ninane's plot began to brew even as Dugan's fingers began to draw circles on her inner thigh.

"Tut tut, Ninane. Jealousy doesn't become you. I promised Aoife your face would not be seen near their *sithein* and you'll be sure to keep my word. Leave it be. There are other plots to be made on other days but this one is over."

"Yes, yes of course," she replied absently as he found just what he'd been looking for.

Chapter Seven

Haley walked along the beautiful sidewalks near their home, smiling at what she saw. Her mother-in-law moved beside her, leaving a warm flow of magic in her wake.

Dana was a teacher of magic and she'd been spending a great deal of time with Haley, tutoring her, schooling her on basic skills. Haley might have been embarrassed to be with the very young Faerie children but in truth, using her magic was so wonderful, so fun it didn't matter all that much.

"Have you given much thought as to what you plan to do? I mean for the next little while at least?" Dana hesitated. "I don't mean to push but I know my son. I've seen how he is with you. It's good. But I can't lie and tell you I don't mind if he's not around."

Haley nodded. "I understand. You must resent me at least a little. You wouldn't have this uncertainty if I weren't around." It was difficult, trying to find her place in the *sithein*. They'd all known each other for centuries at least and she was a total newcomer. Like the first day at a new school.

Dana stopped, taking Haley's hands in her own. "We don't resent you at all. You have no idea how happy we are for Conall now that he's found you. Having him back is joyous, but you were a surprise. One I wasn't sure about until I'd spent a few moments with you and realized why he loves you."

Haley laughed. "The bond?"

"Haley, yes, the bond ties you together but you're free to make of that what you will. It can be easy or difficult, passionate or bland and mildly comfortable. You two are magic together. And you manage him well."

A tiny knot in her belly eased. It wasn't as if Haley had a terrible family life. She loved her parents even if they had kept this secret from her. Still, being held in affection and regard by the people most important to Conall meant something to Haley. A big something.

"My parents aren't immortals." Haley shrugged. "I can't be here full time because I don't have a lot of time left with them. So I'll need to go and visit them often. Originally, I planned to keep my job at the Foundation but right now, I need to focus on being here and I don't feel like I can give them the time my old job demands."

Dana smiled, putting a hand to Haley's cheek for a moment. "I know you must miss your parents a lot. Your grandmother knows she's welcome here any time? Your parents are too. You'd have to guide them in and out but if they wanted to come here for a while, we have plenty of room in our home. And, well, I hope you know Cormac and I think of you as one of our own so if you need me, need a mother or a shoulder, please come to me. I'd be honored."

"Thank you. My grandmother does know and I expect she'll visit from time to time. My parents? It's complicated but I'll be sure they know the offer is open. I do appreciate it and your kindness to me as well." Haley knew her mother would most likely not be visiting at all. She hoped things would ease over time but she wouldn't hold her breath.

Dana squeezed her shoulder and they continued to walk until they heard someone call out to them.

"Hello there!" Conall's sister Aideen called out as they passed. Haley quite liked the way her new family's houses tended to be clustered along the walk from the school to Haley and Conall's home. Inside the *brugh* was like a Faerie township. Neighborhoods, town squares, shops. Haley loved that even though the Fae could magic whatever goods they wanted or needed, they still appreciated and sought out handcrafted goods.

It wasn't middle America, the world inside the hill was more exotic with houses of every shape and description. Flowers and trees, many the same or similar to those outside but some in colors Haley had no words for.

They'd stopped at Aideen's hail so Haley turned her attention to her sister-in-law. The sable-haired woman who looked a great deal like her mother waved at them. "Come through and have a cup of tea. Auntie is here."

While she liked her mother-in-law a great deal, it was hard to fit into their very large, close-knit family even though they'd gone out of their way to make Haley feel welcome. Aideen was, well, very nosy and clearly her brother could do no wrong. At first Haley had been very charmed by that, but after a while, it began to get on her nerves. But she did like and connect with Aoife, so she went in to visit for a few hours until the sun began to set and she needed to get home and said her goodbyes.

"I will walk a while with you, then. I would like to speak with you about something." Aoife stood and accompanied Haley out and up the hillside toward her and Conall's home.

"I sense you're feeling a bit at loose ends."

"I guess you're queen because you get right to the point."

Aoife laughed. "I do enjoy you so much, Haley. I'm a forward person, it suits me and I think it suits you as well. You're learning how to use your magic with Dana and I'd like to offer you something as well."

"What?"

Aoife stopped just shy of the front gate where tendrils of vines, heavy with flowers, hung and scented the air.

"You're a descendant of Macha and I've got a few skills as a warrior. I thought we could put those things together and see if you'd be amenable to some training for battle and fighting."

Haley snorted in disbelief. "A *few* skills? Modesty does not suit you at all. You're renowned for your skills as a warrior and a trainer of other warriors. There are odes written about you! When Conall told me you were his aunt I was shocked you actually existed outside legend. I'd be honored to train with you. But what makes you think it's something for me?"

"As I said, you're one of Macha's." Aoife shrugged. "She's of the earth, which is why your magic is so strong and elemental. Like me, she's renowned for battle and war. You and I should be a powerful force, I think. I trained Cormac you know. That's how he met Dana to begin with."

Something clicked into place inside Haley as she imagined being trained for battle. She'd never even considered it before but it intrigued her. "As I said, I'd be honored. Dana is teaching me how to manage my magic and Rhona is teaching me Fae history. So much I don't know." The loneliness and feeling of being out of place swelled for a moment.

Aoife touched her cheek briefly and smiled. "You feel like an outsider. It must be hard. This *sithein* has stood for twenty thousand years. We all know each other and ourselves too. You miss your home and you wish to visit?"

Haley nodded, tears suddenly in her eyes. Aoife peered into Haley's face and the tears eased as Haley felt *understood*.

"You should go then. Go and tend to your human family for a time and come back. This will be your home but that doesn't mean you have to cut off your other life. Conall will be..." Aoife hesitated, "...difficult when it comes to letting you come and go. It's partly because of what he suffered and the fact that Ninane is still out there. And partly because of who he is. He's a prince and despite being an intellectual, he's a very forceful man used to getting his way."

"That's a very diplomatic way of saying he's a control freak."

Aoife laughed. "I've found, over many years of life, males like Conall tend to make it worth your while in the end."

"At least once or twice a day." Haley winked, feeling better for the levity. "So can I tell Conall you said it was okay for me to go back and see my family? Dana and I discussed this earlier today as well. If I had his mother and his aunt behind me, he might be easier to convince."

Aoife shook her head. "Go on now, he loves you. I'm sure he'll want you to be happy. Come to me when you return and we can begin to train. And Haley? Do be careful. Ninane isn't to be trifled with." She pressed a kiss to Haley's cheek and turned to meander along the flowers, her sweetness as well as her warning, hanging in the air.

Conall heard the front door slide open and automatically moved to meet her in the entry. Her eyes brightened when she caught sight of him and it lightened his heart. Loved the shape of her in a short, summery dress and sandals, her hair free, light dancing on her face.

"Hello there, Irish witch. And how are you today?" He kissed her, meaning just a brief touch of lips but the need he had for her rushed back to life, roaring through him until there was nothing but her and wanting to touch her everywhere.

She opened her mouth, letting him in and the warmth of

her stole over him. She met his fever with her own, writhing against his body like she couldn't get enough. A soft moan broke from her, filling his mouth.

His hands ripped at her dress, pulling the hem up to expose her pussy as he backed her against the wall, all the while continuing to kiss her. An arm around her waist took the impact when their bodies met the wall.

"Sweet Lady, you're so wet," he gasped, wrenching his mouth free when his fingers slid beneath her panties and into her pussy.

She arched her back and rolled her hips, taking him deeper where she was hot as well as slick. "Please, make me come. I need you, Conall."

Longing escaped through his lips, low and insistent as he dropped to his knees before her. He made quick work of her panties and pressed his face to her, still against her body for long moments as he let his body remember she was *his.*

Her fingers combed through his hair, tracing over the tips of his ears, sending echoes of sensation down his spine and around to his cock. Her scent wove through him, grabbing him in her spell.

Quickly, he placed her thigh on his shoulder and his mouth found her pussy, tongue pressing against her clit, feeling her pulse there as it played against his own.

While his fingers fucked into her, he devoured her. Licking slowly through the furls of her cunt over and over until her breath rushed from her in short gasps. Her taste on his tongue was heaven, there was nothing better in the universe than her honey.

The walls of her pussy began to flutter around his invading fingers and he put his lips around her clit and sucked, flicking his tongue against the sensitive underside relentlessly.

A low cry vibrated through her as she came, her fingers tightening in his hair, holding him against her pussy as she bloomed, her honey scalding against his mouth and hands.

Before she'd even stopped coming, Haley found herself on her hands and knees in the entry of their home, Conall's body just behind her as she heard the rasp of his zipper.

"I'm going to fuck you now, Haley. The scent of you is driving me wild." His voice was little more than a growl as he ran his hands over the cheeks of her ass, fingers finding her gate, playing for a few moments until she was nearly ready to beg again.

But when the head of him met that slick flesh, she sighed and pushed back to take him into her body, glorying at the feel of his cock filling her as she stretched to accommodate him.

She'd never felt so consumed by anything before and yet, every time he touched her she wanted him inside her body. If she was upset, his touch calmed her even as that fire began to stoke low. His body next to hers in their bed every night belonged there and she knew it with total certainty.

"Lady, so tight. Hot and tight. I think I may die from your cunt."

Haley's eyes slid closed as she let herself feel his need, his adoration and love for her in the way his hands caressed the line of her spine, tested the heaviness of her breasts through the bodice of the dress he'd ripped open in his need to touch her right then.

Her nipples hardened even further as he palmed them and then rolled and tugged.

His cock slid through her body, invading and retreating. The sounds of fucking echoed against her soft gasps and moans. One hand left her nipple and slid down her belly, finding her clit.

"Fuck. I love the way you tighten around me when I touch your clit. Such a hungry pussy and all mine," he whispered in her ear before flicking his tongue over the tip in time with his thrusts and the movement of his middle finger over her clit. How he could keep a rhythm was beyond her, so she didn't think about anything other than how good he made her feel.

His body against her back caged her, anchored her as he brought her to a climax so hard and deep she felt as if she exploded from her lower gut in a burst of white-hot pleasure.

Leaving her clit behind, his fingers dug into her hip to hold her as he straightened and drove into her body hard and fast. She held on to the bottom stair near her head and pushed back against him, taking him deeply.

The edge of his control was sharp, she felt it as he leashed it only barely. A thrill ran through her that she tested him so greatly and small aftershock orgasms skittered through her pussy as he thrust deep one last time and came with a low groan of her name.

"You're amazing," he whispered, pressing a kiss to her shoulder before slipping out of her body.

"I'm amazing? Conall, you tongued my ear, fingered my clit and fucked me in the same rhythm. *That's* amazing. I can barely walk and chew gum at the same time and you've got all your body parts working in tandem."

He laughed as he helped her up. "On the floor in the hall. You see what you do to me? I can't even wait until I get you to the bedroom." He kissed her and she tasted herself on his lips.

"I like that." She smiled, feeling almost shy. "I like that I make you feel that way."

"Let's get a bath in and then we'll have a meal and fuck again."

"You've got your priorities straight."

He led her upstairs to their ridiculous bathroom. Twice the size of her flat in Ireland, the bathroom was a monument to Fae hedonism. She'd noticed the Fae put just as much, if not more energy into lavish bathrooms than they did their homes. They loved the water but it was more than that.

Conall's bathroom had a shower lined with benches. Multiple showerheads lined the walls at different heights as well as two rain spouts on the ceiling. Deep green marble that surprisingly was not slippery to walk on made the space seem even more decadent. That and the greenery that hung from the ceiling and made up the wall between the entry to the shower and the rest of the bathroom.

It also featured a tub so deep she could stand in it. The jets aimed at naughty places as well as the lower back and shoulders. The ceiling was glass and there were lights set into the walls themselves.

A total experience and there were days Haley was quite sure she'd never want to leave the room. Some days it was about pleasure, others it was about not being able to process every bit of her life that was new and unexpected still.

She bustled around, laying out thick towels and their robes while he started the shower and the tub.

"Ambitious." Haley nodded toward him, loving the way his long hair slid over that tawny skin like a cloak.

"We'll shower first and then have a soak. I've got some lovely riseberry wine all chilled and ready for that portion of the evening. You can drink it while I eat your pussy again."

And like that, her body roared to life once more, making him chuckle in that knowing, masculine way.

She took the hand he held out and let him pull her into the shower.

"Did you have a good day today?" he asked as she washed her hair.

Haley told him about the things his mother had taught her that day at the school. The pride on his face warmed her.

"She's a good teacher, my mother. She tells me you're a natural with a lot of power. Aoife tells me the same."

"Speaking of Aoife, she's offered to have me start battle training with her. When I return." She rinsed off and gave in to his soap-slicked hands as he ran them between her legs. "How can I talk to you when you do that?"

He sighed but didn't argue. "You need to go home. To deal with your job and see your parents. I assume I'm welcome to come as well?"

"Just like that?" Haley had expected a fight from him.

"I don't like it. But how can I deny you a wish to see your parents when I know what it is to miss mine so much? In many ways, I'm glad I couldn't feel all those centuries. The ache of missing them for even those brief hours after the spell was broken and before we came back was staggering. I hate seeing you sad. I do hope you'll want to be here most of the time."

His fingers began to tease her clit, tease an orgasm from her and she grabbed his wrist. "Wait," she gasped. "I want to talk right now. You're trying to distract me. Yes, of course, you're welcome. I'd like you to meet my parents. I need to quit my position and get my things together. I'll also have to work something out with my grandmother so that when I'm here, she can contact me if something is up with my family."

"We can be on their doorstep in a matter of moments once we leave the *sithein* but we'll be sure your grandmother has the spell to find the door here and we can lay wards at her house and your parents' house so if there's any extreme emotion like pain or grief it'll alert you here. You're all right then? With staying here most of the time?"

He turned off the shower and led her to the tub which steamed nicely. She stepped in, sat on the bench and let her legs dangle in the water. The weightlessness and the heat of the water stole over her, relaxing her into a nearly inebriated state.

"Yes. I like your family. I like it here. I'm Fae, I belong here." Her voice sounded dreamy even to her own ears. "I'm suspicious at how easy you're taking this."

First a chuckle from him and then the cork on the special oil Conall used in the bath popped. It made the water perfect for making love. He often used his magic to create a small water-free bubble around her gate so he could fuck her comfortably but the water still heated the rest of her. The man was a genius really.

Conall moved to stand in front of her. She opened her thighs to him, as she always did. He kissed her long and slow. Taking his time as he tasted her.

In truth she was right to be suspicious. He hated the idea of her leaving the *sithein*. She was in a lot more danger in the human realm. Vulnerable to whatever in hell Ninane had planned. The bitch had been sighted just a few days prior, although he hadn't mentioned it to Haley yet. There within the gates of the *brugh* he could protect Haley. The protection of the tribe extended to her. Conall had power, true. He was old and came from a noble line. But Haley was new and young and it panicked him to even contemplate what Ninane could do if she got her hands on Haley.

Conall had had his argument to keep Haley within the *sithein* at all times ready for when the inevitable happened and Haley wanted to leave. But his father had come to visit him earlier that day and Cormac had warned his son not to be autocratic with Haley, urging him to pick his battles with her accordingly.

Conall knew his father was right. Haley was strong-willed and would not be controlled or bossed about. Despite her lack of true understanding of the threat she faced, Conall knew he couldn't keep her from the people she loved without creating a rift between them. He'd have to find a way to manage it the best he could and if he was agreeable, he could be there with her at all times. Her agreement to live there in their home most of the year made him very happy indeed. It meant she embraced their life together and her identity as not only his wife but as Fae.

"What are you up to, Conall? You've got that crafty, faraway look."

He grinned, realizing his mouth had drifted from her lips and he stood mere inches away from her as he'd plotted.

"I'm thinking of just how I'll ravish you. On your knees, facing away from me. Hands on the side of the tub."

She obeyed and even kneeling, the water still came to right above her breasts. Moments later he held a soft blindfold he quickly tied on. A surprised but interested sound came from her.

"Now, be quiet and let me pleasure you."

She laughed softly but said nothing.

He hadn't used his magic on her to its full extent yet. That would change right then.

Concentrating, he imagined himself licking and sucking her nipples and sent that to her. Her gasp told him the spell worked. He then imagined taking long, slow licks through the folds of her pussy as he held a vibrator against her pubic bone. No direct clitoral stimulation with it but enough that it would resonate through her, teasing her senses.

A quick bit of magic to hold the water away from the entrance to her cunt and he thrust his cock deep while he slowly tickled her rear passage, not quite entering it.

"Oh," she moaned softly as he fucked her. He grabbed a handful of her hair and directed her head so he could kiss her ears.

"Let me control your senses, darlin'. If you let me in I promise to make it worth your while. Open yourself."

He felt her inner shields fall and flowed in, holding back her orgasm as he worked her higher.

In her mind, he thrust his cock into her mouth and her pussy, filling her doubly with him. Her senses trembled at the intensity of what he gave her as her inner walls heated and squeezed his cock. Her pussy was the wettest he'd ever experienced slipping around him while her hips churned. Small, helpless sounds of pleasure echoed through the room as she let him take her over and fuck every part of her system.

"Yes, Haley. You're so fucking hot for me right now. Your pussy is so wet. Can you feel my mouth on your clit, my fingers barely pressing into your sweet little ass?"

She hissed as he sent her that sensation, tilted her hips so he knew she liked it.

"You like that. Mmmm, Haley, you're a very naughty girl when you want to be. You taste so good, your clit is hard against my tongue. You want to come, don't you?"

She cried out what sounded like a desperate yes. He added mouths sucking on the tips of her ears and teeth abrading her nipples. Her breath shuddered and her entire body trembled.

He let go of his control, letting her climax wash over her. She sucked in her breath and her head whipped back. Her cunt clamped down around him as she shook, the water lapping over her skin and his. It was such an erotically beautiful sight that, coupled with her pussy sucking greedily at his cock, he let his own orgasm take over.

He picked her up gently and dried her off with magic. The scent of dinner reached her as he laid her on their bed.

"Do I have to eat?" she mumbled, not wanting to open her eyes. She'd never felt anything like what he'd done to her in the bathtub before. So much sensation it nearly drowned her. Every cell in her body was sated and she stretched, lazy as a cat in a sunny window.

"You do." He kissed the tip of her nose. "Come on then. Open your eyes. Here's a glass of wine. We forgot to drink it in the bath." He laughed in that sexy way he had about him.

An eye cracked open and she had to add the other to take him in. Long dark hair draped about his body, tribal markings on his shoulder and upper arm, arrogant expression firmly lodged on his face that said he knew just how much pleasure he'd given to her.

"You're a very useful man." She winked and sat up to take in the huge spread he'd created for them. "I think I'll keep you around."

"Good. Now eat. You'll need your strength for round three."

Chapter Eight

Haley took a steadying breath as she watched her father through narrowed eyes. He'd agreed to see her for a private lunch near his office. She knew her grandmother must have been in contact with him because he'd plunged right into topics that had nothing to do with anything and so far she'd let him avoid her questions until their food arrived.

Conall sat at a table across the room, refusing to leave her alone with her father. They'd fight about that one later. But his presence was comforting.

She took a bite of her sandwich and sat back. "Okay, cut the crap, Dad. Let's have at it. You know why I wanted to talk to you."

His eyes, as green as hers, widened at her brass for a moment before he sighed and shrugged. "I won't apologize for what I did. I did it for you. Your mother isn't like I was." He looked around quickly. "I couldn't stand the thought of not having her with me and we didn't know what it would do to you even if I hadn't given you my heritage. I would have had to watch you die too. I'm not willing to do that. So I gave you the best thing I had other than my love itself and I don't regret it."

She huffed and took another bite. "You have no right to be so sweet and take the sting out of my ire," she grumbled and he laughed. "You should have told me. You should have asked me first. You gave up everything." And now she was totally different than he was. Alone in their family in her otherness.

"You haven't been listening, Haley Maeve O'Brian. I *have* everything. Your mother is my wife. I love her with all I am. You are my child, I love you with all I am. What I gave up was nothing compared to that. You are protected. You have family after Mom and I pass. You have people who'll be with you forever." Reaching across the table, he took her hand and squeezed it. "I'm losing a lot of it. My memories. Your grandmother says that's the price and while it's sad, it's one I'll pay for your mother and you."

Tears stung her eyes. "I love you so much, Dad. I don't want you to...I don't want to lose you."

"Sweetheart, you'd lose me either way. That's how life works. But I'm your dad no matter what." He tipped his chin toward Conall's table. "Now, are you going to introduce him to me or what? Your mother will have kittens when she finds out I met him first." He laughed, that deep, joyful sound she associated with so many wonderful memories. "What? You thought your grandmother would hold out that gossip? She loves gossip and this is pretty big."

She leaned in and whispered, "Dad, you gave up your life for me. I'm upset about this!"

He waved it away. "Haley, tough shite. I did it. It's done. It was mine to give and I did and you have it and it suits you. Your husband is like you and you'll share your life with him as I've done with Mom. Get over it. Parents do things for their children every day. Anyway, it was selfish too. Now, bring your man over here so I can size him up with my fatherly gaze."

Haley growled as she pushed back and swiveled to make eye contact with Conall to motion him over.

Conall bowed low to her father before sitting next to her.

"Conall macCormac, this is my father, Joseph O'Brian. Dad, this is my husband, Conall."

"It's a pleasure to meet you so that I may thank you for giving me Haley and to assure you she'll always be safe with mine and at my side," Conall said smoothly.

"Hmm. We'll get into more detail about that in private. For now, I'm happy to meet you as well. My mother tells me a number of things, all of which satisfy me but there are things I don't know yet. Let's get this to go. Haley's mother will be pacing a hole in the runner in the entry by now. I promised her we'd deal with this quickly and get home. She's anxious to see you and to meet Conall as well."

Ninane fumed. And plotted. Each time the human witch left the *sithein* was an opportunity to observe. She'd learn and find a way to get at her.

She'd watched as Conall courted the humans who didn't deserve him. Humans were weak but they gave her the perfect leverage. As long as that red-haired human had connections to these weaklings, Ninane had a way to her. Her powers were still weak although Dugan's people hadn't lied when they'd noted her potential. In a few years, if the whore was still alive, her powers would rival Ninane's. But that couldn't be allowed.

It was hard enough to watch him with *her*, the way he looked at her. Even from a cloaked distance, Ninane could see the magic between them, the bond that'd been forged between Conall and the human woman. It glittered, strong and bright. Each day they were together it would only strengthen, making both individually stronger and more resilient as well. The idea of that *thing* bearing Conall's children made Ninane nauseated. And so jealous it sent her into a blind rage every time she thought on it for very long.

Haley lay tucked up against Conall's body in her old bedroom late that night after a very long, involved evening with her parents.

"God, I think my mother has a crush on you." Haley snuggled back into him closer. "Creepy. And, just to add to that weirdness, I think she likes you better. You got the bigger piece of cake. I love cake and you got the corner piece with all the good frosting."

Conall licked up the edge of her ear, making her shiver. "It's impossible to like anyone more than you. They're happy for you. They're very hospitable and once your father was done questioning me and he was satisfied you'd be safe and they could see you any time they wanted, he relaxed."

"I can't believe they didn't even complain when you set up the wards and the trigger spell so they could contact me at home. They flipped out any time magic was even alluded to the whole time I was growing up and now it's all hunky dory." She snorted. Still, Haley noted her mother's general discomfort with anything magical and how she'd shied away from any promises to come to the *sithein* to visit. It made her deeply sad not to be able to share that part of her life with her mother.

"That's a very cool spell by the way. Since we can't get cell service in Faeryland or wherever and all."

"They wanted to protect you until you were ready. And it had to be painful for your father on some level, to know he'd given up his magic. I know you're sad and feeling guilty. Let it go. He doesn't regret it. Let him give this to you and be proud." One of the things she loved so much about Conall was how astute he was about other people.

"I know. I know. I just feel like I've stolen something from him." Haley knew she had to let it go but it was hard.

"He doesn't. Haley, he loves your mother. She's his mate. Not in a metaphysical sense but in every other way. He's given you his love in one way and her his love in another. Let him. Honor him in accepting that."

She sighed, relaxing. "You're right. Thank you. Thank you for helping me and them too."

"Of course. They're my family as well."

He slid questing hands under the hem of her shirt, finding her nipples.

"That is *so* not going to happen with my parents right upstairs!" she whispered.

"Oh yes it is. You'll just have to be very quiet."

One handed, he shoved her pajama pants down her legs, bringing her thigh up on top of his.

"You're the one not wearing panties. What kind of woman doesn't wear panties you might ask? Why, the kind who wants a cock deep inside her pussy, that's who." His lips rested against her ear, his words a mere breath.

"Because you keep stealing them. This is crazy." But with each word she sounded less and less convincing.

"Finger yourself, Haley. I want you nice and primed."

When the man went all *über* sex god like that it melted her and made her crazy. That was the only way to explain her hand sliding down her belly and finding its way to her clit.

"That's it, darlin'." His hand joined hers while the other still rolled and pinched a nipple. Entwining his fingers around hers, he guided her, stroking her clit in unison. "Wet. So wet. Shall we gather some of your honey?" Without waiting for an answer, he guided their hands to her gate and just inside to bring her wetness up and around her clit over and over again until she had to bite her bottom lip to keep from moaning.

His cock slid between her thighs, rubbing over her pussy, brushing against their fingers.

"I need you, Haley. Like breathing. Every time I look at you I want to be inside you."

When orgasm hit, he slid his cock home and began to thrust slowly, silently. He brought their hands to her mouth. "Turn your head."

She did and he brought their fingers between their mouths and he licked them and her lips. As she gasped, her taste exploded through her system, layered with his skin.

He devastated her with the way he wanted her. It made the fear slide away, even for a few minutes. Even if nothing else in her life was certain, he was. *They were.*

"Shhh. Quiet now, we don't want to get caught."

"You're a very, very naughty man," she sighed, arching to take him deeper.

"I am. All for you, Haley." The amusement in his voice caught her, making her want to laugh even as pleasure slid through her system, sinuous and warm.

"What does it feel like? Being inside me?"

"Open to me," he whispered and she let him into her mind. His magic brushed against hers, gently filling her until it was as if she sat inside him instead of the other way around.

So hot. He was right, her pussy was hot and soft inside as it surrounded every part of him in a wet embrace. The pleasure of it was unimaginable to her until that moment. The tingling of his balls as they drew tight against him, the way he could feel her pulse beat within the walls of her body—it was as if he drowned in her in a sense.

Her own pleasure merged with his and she began to come around him and the clench of her inner muscles shot through his cock and up his spine. She felt the approach of his orgasm and when it hit, experienced the burst of pleasure as each pulse of his cock moved within her.

When he withdrew his magic and his body, she lay, utterly spent and happy he'd shared such an intimate thing with her.

"I love you, Haley."

"I love you, too. Thank you for sharing that with me."

"I want to share everything with you. Being buried inside you like that, your body responding to me...I've lived a long, long time, Haley, and nothing compares. It sounds trite to say but you complete me."

"I'm so lucky."

"Would you like to get even luckier?" He insinuated his hips against her.

He was going to kill her.

Conall stared, trying to get her attention but the Irish witch ignored him as she told her boss she'd have to stop working full time but *oh yes, she'd stay on as a Foundation member.* Like hell she would!

"Haley, can I speak with you a moment?"

His wife waved a distracted hand in his direction and mumbled something sounding like *in a minute.* In a minute? There was a crazy Fae out to kill him for good this time and wouldn't pause a moment to harm Haley to get to him and she waved him off?

After another hour they went on. He was sure he'd ground his teeth into nothing while she nattered on excitedly about Foundation business and how they'd transition her from full time into the occasional meeting schedule of a Foundation member.

Finally she looked up, face glowing with pleasure and for half a moment he nearly lost perspective and decided to not be huffy over her change of plans without consulting him.

Instead he took her arm, nodded to her boss and escorted her out. He'd given notice at his job before they'd even left for her grandmother's house that first day after the spell so it was on to Kerry to visit Maeve before heading back to the *brugh*.

He sifted them to a lovely meadow near her gran's home and sat her down, frowning.

"What are we doing here?" She looked around, pretty strands of her hair wafting around in the breeze.

"Don't you act clueless with me. We'd decided you were going to quit altogether and stay within the *sithein*. At least until we'd dealt with Ninane once and for all. You can't mean to continue to come back and forth all the time, Haley. It's not safe and I can't always come and go with you on the drop of the hat. I have a job too."

Her eyebrows flew up in outrage. "I don't need your permission to keep the job I had before I met you, buster! They're doing some work I've been part of planning for two years. I want to be part of the realization of that. And I don't need you to escort me everywhere. I know how to sift now. I'll come straight, just outside the hill and sift directly to my office at the Foundation, to my grandmother's or to my parents. I'll be fine."

"Your dunderheaded assurances that you'll be fine are not comforting to me in the least. We know Ninane has taken refuge below. They won't give her up. She tried to kill me. Do you think she'll stop now that I'm back because she's bored? The script on the scrolls? It's written in my blood, Haley. Do you think I want that to be you?"

Her furrowed brow flattened a bit as she sighed. She

reached out and entwined her fingers with his. "Conall, I understand you're worried about me. I do. And I love that. I'm not a moron and I will make every effort to have you with me when I come out here. But I have a life here as well. My grandmother, my parents, the Foundation are all very important to me and I won't give that up. I can travel to them in the blink of an eye. Which means I can see them every few weeks around my building a new life with you in the hill. Don't make it either or. I didn't ask that of you. It's not fair and I won't do it. Anyway, Aoife is going to start training me so I'll be more than equipped to defend myself."

He groaned. He'd thought the training would be a way for his aunt and Haley to bond. He should have known better. Haley had the blood and magic of a warrior queen and his aunt of course *was* a warrior queen. That's what he deserved for thinking with his cock when Haley had told him of the plan.

"Why are you groaning?" Her eyes narrowed and he sensed dangerous ground with *offended female* written all over it.

"I'm just annoyed and worried. Let's go visit your gran and we'll talk more later." He kissed her quickly and she sent him a look that told him she didn't plan to let it go.

"Oh no you don't. You can't give me that look and that suffering man sigh and think you can just bust on over to my gran's house without answering for it."

Lady, he was done for. "Haley, Aoife is a warrior queen. She's been so for tens of thousands of years. She might train you but do you think it'll somehow actually equip you to deal with Ninane in a few weeks?"

"Do I look slow to you? Did I say I'd be all ninja warrior in two weeks? You know, you might be like a million years old and all, but you're a tool sometimes. I'm not stupid. I'm not gullible. But I'm not going to let you wrap me in cotton and put me on a shelf either. I will have to prepare my life for this new stage and as far as I'm concerned, this new stage doesn't equal me sitting around looking pretty until Ninane the crazy Fae gets caught. That's not what I signed on for."

He wisely held back a groan and snort of annoyance. He treasured his balls and he knew she'd punch him if he gave in to those emotions.

"Haley, I don't think you're stupid and I don't expect you to sit around. But you are no match for Ninane! You can't think to flit about like there's no danger. There is. She will kill you without batting an eye. You need to take that seriously."

He stood and began to pace and she joined him, feet apart, eyes blazing, hands on her hips.

"Lookie here, mister man, don't go all fatherly on me. I'm your wife and you don't get to ground me. I do take it seriously but I'm not going to hide for God knows how long it takes to deal with this threat. I'm not going to forego seeing my parents and living my damned life to make you feel better. I'm sorry you're worried. I am. But sorry enough to be extra careful is not sorry enough to sit around and wait to be saved. This discussion is over."

The minx sifted them to her gran's house and thank the Lady, Maeve's house appeared to be bursting at the joints when they arrived. He knew Haley would hold off on the fight until they returned home and hopefully she'd have cooled off by then.

Haley's frustration at Conall fell away when she entered her gran's house and heard the laughter and the language. It wasn't any human language Haley had ever heard but she understood it after a few moments and knew it must be the Traveling Folk.

"Gran?"

Her grandmother met her in the doorway, smiling. "Hello,

sweetheart! Come in. We've been waiting for you and your man." Maeve looked past Haley to Conall and winked. The rogue blew her gran a kiss and strolled in, cuffing an arm around her waist on his way.

A dozen faces looked up, all smiling, as they entered.

"Haley, this is your family."

A tiny woman with hair as bright red as a cardinal's feather stood and enveloped Haley in a hug. "I'm your great-grandmother Rosaleen. It's good to finally be able to hug you like this. We've watched you from afar, kept an eye on you but this is better. You're a lovely girl. You've got your father's eyes. Come in and sit with me and bring your husband with you. He's a handsome one, isn't he? Lucky."

Haley met her great-aunt and a passel of cousins as well. They talked, shared their lives with her, asked her questions of their own, quizzed Conall and charmed Haley to the point of tears. She'd missed so much not being a part of this as she'd grown up.

They secured her promise to come and stay with them in the fall for Samhain so they could have a wedding feast for her and Conall and she could meet the rest of her people.

"There are more?" Haley sat on her gran's couch, leaning back into Conall after a very satisfying supper.

Her great-grandmother laughed. "Sweet girl! There are hundreds more. We don't move as much as we used to. I leave that to the younger folk. But you've got many cousins, second and third even. They'll all love to welcome you both."

"And you should all be welcome at the *brugh* of my people as well. I'll leave word at the door to admit you and yours," Conall said in that charming Irish brogue of his. She hadn't forgotten he'd called her dunderheaded earlier that day, even if he was warm and smelled good.

They talked on and on into the wee hours of the morning until Haley and Conall finally said their goodbyes and sifted back to the *sithein* and walked home. It was very late and very quiet and Haley loved hearing the soft sounds of leaves whispering in the breeze, of water babbling over rocks and tumbling over the small series of falls that led the way around the town.

"It feels like home," she murmured and Conall stopped, bending his head to kiss her fiercely.

"You make it that way, Haley." He looked at her, looked *into* her and her anger melted. Not all of it, but most.

"Mmm, hmm. You're still in trouble. But I'm so tired it's going to have to wait."

Chuckling, he let her lean into him as they walked up the path to their front door and into the house she'd now thought of as home.

Chapter Nine

Sweat trickled down Haley's temple as she went through the drill over and over. The blade in her hand had been forged for her alone by Aoife's master swordcrafter. The weight was perfect for her hand and the balance was magical.

She spun, hearing Aoife's command in her head. Her right foot planted, took her balance and she kicked up with her left, hitting the target before slicing up with the blade.

Her muscles ached, trembled and burned but she began to feel as if she knew what she was about there on that training floor after three months of intensive work.

Aoife was no soft teacher. She was a warrior and she brooked nothing less than every last bit of Haley's effort and concentration. If she wavered for even a moment, Aoife would sweep in and whack her with the wooden sword she'd first trained Haley with.

Haley's softly defined arms and legs had begun to take on a work-hard tone. Her hand-eye coordination had sped. She was sharper, keener, honed.

She'd left to have a board meeting at the Foundation, accompanied by Conall and had visited her parents once and her grandmother as well. Conall never let her go on her own, and each time it started another fight because he made her feel as if she were being selfish for wanting a life outside the *brugh* as well as inside.

"You're not paying attention, Haley."

She ducked, kicking out and knocking Aoife off her feet before the wood connected.

"Very nice!" Aoife laughed as Haley hauled her to her feet.

"I've got enough bruises from that damnable wooden sword of yours."

"Come on then. Let's have a nice soak in the hot springs and we can walk over to dinner together." Aoife didn't even look sweaty. Haley wanted to roll her eyes. The woman looked like a queen every moment of the day. She probably didn't even get morning breath. Still, she'd been a wonderful mentor to Haley and a friend and she made Haley's new life in the *brugh* a lot easier.

Dana, and Conall's sister Aideen joined them for the soak as well as Rhona, Conall's second cousin who worked as an archivist in one of the main libraries in the *brugh*. Haley worked with her a few times a week, finding a great deal of satisfaction in the knowledge the Fae loved history, art and culture as much as she did.

"Auntie tells us you're a natural with a blade," Aideen said lazily as steam wafted up from the water's surface.

Without vanity, Haley felt that to be true. Not that she was a super hero or anything, but her blood ran in a line known for prowess in battle and those drills felt natural, *right*. Still, she answered cautiously because she'd come to realize Aideen frequently had an agenda. There was an Aideen in every family.

"I hear you'll be starting with horses tomorrow. I can't wait to see that one. It's all Cormac can talk about." Dana laughed. Haley's father-in-law was a master horseman and they had connected over a love of horses and riding. He'd be in charge of her training on horseback.

"If it keeps her here more often, Conall will stop being so grouchy, I hope." Aideen sighed dramatically.

"Don't go there, Aideen. Your brother is illogical and unreasonable over my movements outside the *brugh* and I won't have it. I don't have to explain myself for wanting to see my family." Haley knew she sounded defensive but it was a point she was bone tired of making.

"He gets worried about you. After they saw Ninane in the valley last month he's been worse. If you could just stay here until it passes, things would be smoother."

Haley sighed and looked at Aideen. "Smoother for whom? Would *you* stop seeing your parents because of some threat we don't even know will ever stop? I understand your taking his side, you're his sister. But when he got his magic back I came here with him. I helped him get to you, his family, and I don't appreciate anyone standing between me and my family." She stood. "I'll see you all later at dinner. I'm not feeling very social right now."

"Please don't rush off," Dana called after her.

"It's all right. I need to go for now. I'll see you all in a few hours." Haley left before anyone could follow, heading home.

Conall waited for her in their living room, looking lean and sexy in jeans and a T-shirt. Most of the time the two of them wore modern, human clothing though he'd reverted to wearing the braids and beads that marked his status at his temples and she always wore the necklace her grandmother had given her.

"I hear you had words with my sister," he said without preamble as she entered and the bit of peace she'd enjoyed at coming home fizzled away.

It shouldn't have annoyed her as much as it did but Christ, the woman was a nosy one.

"Of course you did. Not that anyone could let it lie. What, did she run over here to beat me home?" Haley tossed herself on their overstuffed couch and looked up at him.

"She's my sister, it's a matter of a very simple communication spell here within the *sithein*. I don't like that you're upset with my family."

"And I don't like that I've given up everything to be here with you and that's still not enough. I don't like not even being able to take a fucking soak in the hot springs without your busybody sister nosing into my private business. Or it *would* be private if you hadn't chosen to share it with all and sundry."

"Don't be insulting, Haley." His voice was calm as he attempted to soothe her and that just pissed her off further.

"Don't try and patronize me, Conall. I'm in a bad mood and I'm not going to back down. Leave me the hell alone for a while." She sighed and stood, making to leave but he blocked her.

"I'm not patronizing you. You came in, insulted my sister and are currently trying to pick a fight. What is wrong with you?" Anger and frustration marred his features.

"Oh you can fuck right off, you Fae asshat! I walked in the door to our home and immediately find out your sister has run to tattle on me. And not for the first time, I might add. I'm trying to leave the room to *avoid* a fight but you won't move. Do you need to contact Aideen to ask her if I can leave the room?"

"You're out of line."

"Yes, yes I am and you put me there. Let me ask you something, Conall. Did you tell Aideen our life wasn't her business?"

"What is your problem? No, I didn't insult my sister by refusing her inquiry. That's not even the context of the conversation we had. She was upset you'd left the way you had. She wanted to be sure you were all right. I thought you liked my sister." He threw his hands up.

"If she was concerned about me, she could have contacted *me*. She tattled. I'm over it. I'd appreciate it, if you can't keep your damned mouth shut about our business to your sister, if you'd not include me in it. God knows we'd never want to upset Aideen. After all, she's your wife. Oh wait, no she isn't. I am. Silly me. Let me leave, Conall, and we don't have to go through this. Because we've gone through it enough and I'm sick to death of it."

"We can't go to dinner with you like this!"

The man was out of his mind. As if she'd go to dinner with them right now. "You're right. So you go on and have a great time. I'm sure you can unload all our personal business, whatever you haven't already, on them and get sympathy. Poor Conall, his wife wants to be able to visit her family and have a job instead of waiting on him whenever he decides to pay attention."

"Haley, wait a damned minute. I don't deserve all this ire." He hauled her to his body and she resisted his physical allure. "I haven't unloaded our personal business on anyone. It's not like that."

"What is it like then, Conall? Your sister actually had the balls to tell me to stay here and not see my family to make it *smoother* for you. How did she know you were upset about my leaving to see my parents and grandmother if you didn't tell anyone? You make it clear every time what a terrible burden I am for wanting more than living my life through you. You clearly tell your family about it. You clearly share it with your friends as well. Mal tried to talk to me about it last week and Dev the week before."

He moved to the couch, pulling her down with him, keeping a firm hold. If she'd wanted to, she could have broken it with magic or physically but she didn't want to escalate the situation. It was precarious enough as it was but she'd had enough and it had to be said.

"Haley, I love you. You're not a burden to me. You're precious to me. I adore you. I want you safe. It drives me crazy to know you leave the safest place anywhere and expose yourself to Ninane's machinations. Aideen just wanted to help in her own way. I know she didn't mean to upset you. She'd be sick if she knew we'd been fighting."

"Poor Aideen. Gosh, well then, I'll give up everything to make her feel better. Oh and you too. Because after all, *you've* got a family and friends, and *you've* got the career you love so much, and *you've* got people to talk to when you're upset. Why do I need any of that when you're happy?" Haley hadn't realized the depth of anger and hurt she'd been feeling until the words had started pouring out. How lonely she'd been for her old life. Yes, she'd been carving out a new life there, slowly making friends and finding her place in the *brugh* but she didn't have friends she could go down the pub with or whom she could call and bitch about her nosy sister-in-law to. She missed that.

"Are you so unhappy then, Haley?" Conall's voice went soft, thick with emotion. "Has this been a lie? Our home and the life we've made or I thought we were making?"

Tears burned her eyes as she shook her head. "No. No it's not a lie. I love you, Conall. But I gave up a lot to be here with you and I don't ask for a whole lot except to see my parents and Gran and attend a meeting here and there. I've been here nearly four months and I've left just a few times. I have no close friends. I have no family of my own. I hate feeling like a burden because I want that comfort every once in a while."

He rained kisses over her face. A thousand tiny presses of his lips over her closed eyes, her cheeks, lips and chin. A desperate sound broke from him, from deep within his body and he rolled them off the couch and onto the floor, his body taking the cushion of the fall as he then rolled atop her.

She opened her eyes to find him looking at her. "I love you, Haley. I can't stand thinking you're unhappy. All I want is you. You safe. You happy. I'm sorry you're not feeling happy."

"I *am* happy, Conall. Okay, not that you're telling everyone our business. But with you and me. With this life. I need my old life too. You have that and I don't get why you resent me having it."

He reached between them and ripped the front of her shirt open, popping the catch on her bra to expose her breasts to his hands. Breathless, she arched into his touch as he growled, grinding his cock into her.

"I don't! Haley, I want you to be happy and fulfilled! I hate the thought of you being unsafe. There is a difference, you know."

He licked up the column of her neck and nibbled the edge of her ear.

"You can't lock me up and expect me to be happy. I can be safe and still have a life. I don't want to live on a shelf. I can't. You have to ease up your hold. I can't live this way, it'll eat at me—at us."

She widened her thighs and rolled her hips.

"Well, I like to eat you, but I know that's not what you mean. It's hard for me, Irish witch. I love you so much. I lived nearly a thousand years without a soul. Never feeling connected to anyone or anything. I have you now, everything has changed. I can't stand the thought of losing it."

She felt the cool air on her bare legs and realized he'd spelled her pants off. The brush of his hard muscled thighs against the inside of her softer ones meant he'd gotten rid of his own as well.

"We're going to fight about this until Ninane is dead. You know that, don't you? I can't help it and it doesn't mean I don't want you to have a life or that I feel you're a burden. I want to protect you. It's how I'm wired."

How he managed to say it all as he kissed his way down her neck and caught both nipples intermittently between his teeth was just a testament to his talent.

"We'll take this up later." She moaned as he sucked hard on her nipple, sending shivers through her.

"I thought we were done."

"Oh please! We are so not done. But you're distracting me and I'm not going to stop you now."

What else did the bloody woman need to fight about? Blood pounded in Conall's ears as the need took over his system. Her scent, as her body warmed, rose between them. Lady, he had to have her right then.

Reaching between their bodies as he kissed and licked over her beautifully sensitive nipples, his fingers found her pussy wet and hot for him. He slid two fingers into her gate, loving the way she moaned and arched.

He rolled, bringing her body atop his and his fingers deep. She pushed back into his hand as her palms supported her weight, resting on his shoulders.

Goddess, he loved it when she was all sexuality like that. When she took what she wanted and lost herself in the way he made her feel.

"Not fingers. Your cock, please." Haley arched and sat back, reaching around and grabbing him.

He hissed. It felt so good when she did that. But then,

nothing as good as the way it felt as the head of his cock sank into her pussy.

Looking up at her, that red hair around her shoulders, the creamy, pale skin, the high, rounded breasts jiggling seductively, he came home. Every time with her it was this way.

Hot, tight and wet, she descended, her pussy taking his cock, hugging it and then releasing it as she rose again. The shirt he'd ripped open hung in a way that showcased her upper body. Her nipples darkened as he rolled them between his fingers.

He would not lose her. Period. But that meant letting her have more freedom because he didn't want to lose her emotionally either.

He needed Haley like he needed to breathe.

"Reach down and spread yourself open for me," he commanded, loving the way her pupils widened a moment as the breath caught in her throat.

She obeyed though, opening herself up, exposing the dark pink of her pussy. His mouth watered. Her clit was swollen, glistening with her honey.

"Fuck. Haley, your cunt is the most beautiful thing."

She moaned, swiveling herself down onto his cock, sending all thought skittering out of his brain for several long moments.

He sent her the feeling of a tongue sliding over her clit, gently at first and then with more pressure and speed as she picked up her pace on him.

Her thighs trembled as her fingers dug into his shoulders. The wall of pleasure building within him threatened to break.

"So close, aren't you, Irish witch? I can feel your pussy all around me. If my mouth really was on your cunt right now, I know you'd be slicker, creamier, your clit hardening. Do you like the way that feels? Flicking against you? I can taste you on my tongue when I close my eyes. Mmmm. Nothing tastes like you."

"God you're good," she gasped out right as she began to come around him. And not a moment too soon as he followed on her heels.

She slumped over his body, breathing heavy as their hearts sped.

Haley stood on still-shaky legs and smiled down at him, all rumpled and sexy. "You know, it's a sin to look so damned good even after all that exertion."

He stood and hugged her, kissing her forehead before releasing her. "You did all the work."

"Your magic did a lot. I prefer the real thing, but that multi-tasking magic tongue working with your cock is pretty handy." She put her hand over his heart, the steady thump against her palm reassured her. "I'm going to take a long bath, listen to music and read. I'll see you later."

"What do you mean? We need to be at dinner in about twenty minutes."

Haley sighed. "I told you I wasn't going. I'll see your mother and your aunt tomorrow. Oh and your father too, he and I will be starting our training on horseback in the morning. But for now, I've had as much of your family as I can take for one day."

"I can't believe you'd do this. It's very petty, Haley."

Her mouth dropped open as she stepped away from his embrace. "Fuck you too. Don't wake me when you get home."

She took her bath but locked the door after slamming it, underlining her desire not to be disturbed. Jerk. Still, she couldn't deny it hurt when she heard the front door close a few minutes later without his saying goodbye.

He still hadn't come home by midnight when she finally gave up and put her book aside. She'd considered sifting out to see her friends for a while but *that,* while it would have been fun and comforting, would have been petty and unsafe. It hurt to have him think her need to not be around his sister after she'd pulled that shit, would be petty. Everyone needed some space to cool off sometimes. Which is why she went to sleep instead of waiting up to yell at him.

Chapter Ten

Ninane sat on a rise with the rocks shielding her, and watched Cormac ride horses with Conall's human whore. Hate and resentment surged through Ninane as she watched *her* ride like a natural.

She was one of Macha's, they'd told Ninane as she'd enquired around about this human woman who'd sealed the bond with Conall. Not only did Conall share her bed and not Ninane's, but Aoife had taken her under her wing. Everything Ninane had ever wanted and the bitch had just walked in and had it handed to her.

All those years before, she'd thought that by pushing Conall to betray Aoife, he'd realize how powerful Ninane was and move his allegiance to her instead of his aunt. Ninane hadn't wanted to hurt Conall, not until he'd spurned her affection and offers. He'd rejected her while seeking his pleasure with woman after woman. But never her for more than a fleeting moment here and there. Why?

Ninane was more beautiful than the woman below on that horse. Her line was older. She was born a Fae and of this tribe and because of this former human, Ninane had to stand and watch from afar as the human took what was rightfully hers.

After a few centuries, Ninane realized she'd *overreacted* a bit with Conall's curse. Conall's refusal to be seduced by her, aside from some lovely sessions in her bed, had vexed her. Ninane could not understand his loyalty to a woman whose throne he could have occupied alongside Ninane—after they'd killed Aoife and then Dugan of course. And speaking of Dugan, she'd promised the information to him and he'd been very displeased she hadn't been able to retrieve it.

She'd handled it all wrong. She realized that now and after she'd watched him with the red-haired bitch, Ninane saw she'd need to change her approach once she got rid of her problem.

Still, every time she caught sight of Conall, he stirred her. In addition to knowing when they left into the human realm, Ninane had some assistance in breaching the *sithein* at least in the outermost areas. Watching Conall was exquisite torture. His long dark hair moving in the breeze, the laughing eyes. His voice, still so sexy. But the way he watched *her* infuriated Ninane. If she couldn't have him, why should this Haley creature?

It was time to deal with the problem. She'd waited long enough to claim Conall and that throne.

"Go ahead and say it." Haley continued to brush down her horse after she and her father-in-law had returned to the stables.

Cormac chuckled as he put away the gear. Haley admired that he did the work himself instead of handing the horses off to stable hands. Haley preferred to do the work herself as well, liked the way it created a relationship with the horse. This mare was new to her, a pretty gray with white socks. Her name was Dulce. Spanish for sweet. And she was that, but with a nice iron will as well. Dulce would suit her just fine.

"Sweetness, I've been married a very long time. Let's see, four thousand years as a matter of fact. My wife is a lovely woman but she's a princess. Bull headed. Used to getting her own way. Conall takes after his mother."

Haley led Dulce back to her stall, made sure she had plenty of water and left her to rest.

"And so you think I should just accept Conall's protective nature and stay here to make it smoother for him."

He took her hand, placing it around his elbow as they began to walk back toward the town.

"No. As a matter of fact, I don't. Conall loves you and yes, he wants to protect you and keep you here where you're safest. But Aideen, well-meaning as she is, was wrong to butt into your personal business with her brother and her brother needs to realize you're a warrior as much as his aunt and I are and you can handle yourself. More than that, you're not meant to be wrapped up and kept. Not and be happy."

Haley looked up at him, surprised. "I didn't expect that. I apologize for misjudging you." She hesitated a moment. "I don't want to upset him. Or anyone else in your family. I don't want to have every action examined and found wanting. I am safe, or as safe as I can be. I know she's out there. But she's here too from what we know. If I give in, next thing I know he'll want me to stay at home because it's even safer."

He smiled. "Haley, you're a spirited woman. You're good for my son. He's had his own way for most of his life. It's hard for him to be thwarted. Even though I believe his motives are good ones, I think you have every right to want to come and go as long as you're thinking about safety. Which from every indication I have, you are."

They paused at the path where it split. One way leading to her home, the other leading to his. "Thank you, Cormac. I appreciate everything you've said."

"Give him some time to cool off. He'll be all right. He's never been afraid to lose anything before. Puts a man in a right state to have something worth losing. You're welcome at ours for lunch you know."

"I do. But I'm going home for now. I have some reading to finish and I'm meeting Rhona down the pub for a pint. I thought it would be nice to get out."

He grinned. "Rhona is a good one. My cousin's third girl. You may see Riordan down there too. He's due back today or tomorrow."

"Ah, this is your oldest son? Conall has been talking of him nonstop."

"Yes, they're very close, those two. He was devastated when Conall went missing. He's been out of touch for the last six months, a part of his job in the human realm. Dana only heard yesterday that he'd be returning home but we decided to keep Conall's return a surprise. I'm sure the moment he enters the *sithein* he'll know."

"Conall will be thrilled. I'm so happy he's got you all."

"As do you, Haley. You're ours as he is. Don't forget that." He winked.

She kissed Cormac's cheek and headed home. The house was quiet. Conall had gotten up and left without saying a word to her and she'd let it go. What else could she do? He knew her feelings.

So she cleaned up and changed before finishing up some files she needed to look over and then headed down the local pub, about a mile from the house.

Most Fae walked everywhere within the *sithein*. For longer distances they might choose to ride horses but inside, the *brugh* was a relatively small town. Haley figured about eight or so square miles and most of the population lived within a mile of the center square. There were doorways to other *sitheins* scattered within the hill as well.

Haley made her way to the Hen and Feather, one of two public houses in the *brugh* and her personal favorite. When Conall had brought her the first time, she'd expressed amazement a pub existed in a Faerie hill. He'd laughed and asked if she'd expected them to be playing harps, drinking out of flowers and thinking really hard all the time.

Whatever she might have imagined, it wasn't that the Fae would have an existence very much like humans had only with less technology and more magic.

Rhona waved from her seat at the long, beautifully polished bar and Haley hopped up next to her. "Hello there."

"And hello yourself. I took the liberty of ordering you a Beamish even though I cannot believe you don't drink Guinness." Rhona tipped her chin to the dark, thick brew in the pint glass in front of Haley.

"Mmmm. Thank you." Haley had also given up thinking it was funny the Fae drank Harp and Guinness as well as Beamish and Murphy's. She'd assumed they'd have their own brands but Conall had scoffed and told her why invent their own brand when Guinness existed?

Rhona sighed heartily and rapped her knuckles on the bar before saying, "So you know Aideen is a nosy so-and-so, don't you?"

Haley laughed. "Straight to the point you go."

"What's the point in wasting time with pleasantries? We both know it needed to be said. She's not a bad girl, our Aideen. She's always busy with her nose up other people's business. She was that way when she was small too. She idolizes her big brother and he can do no wrong. I'm sorry she chased you off last night. Even sorrier Conall came to dinner riled like a bear."

"I wouldn't know. He came home after I'd gone to sleep and

got up and out when I was showering this morning."

"Oh men. Such babies." Rhona winked and Haley laughed. She'd missed this sort of banter. "You know, Haley, I was so glad you asked me to come have a pint with you. I've wanted us to be friends but you seemed so overwhelmed I didn't want to rush up on you and spook you further."

Haley squeezed Rhona's hand. In truth, Haley had realized part of her lack of close friends was her own fault in not really pursuing friendships like she might have in the outside world. If she meant for the *brugh* to be her home, she had to make more of an effort and that prompted her to ask Rhona out to the pub when she saw her earlier.

"Thank you. I've missed having girlfriends. I could have used one last night."

"I thought about showing up at yours with a bottle of wine and something sweet but I didn't want to ruin any make-up sex."

"I appreciate that. So tell me about Dev. I only know him as Conall's friend but the way I see him look at you tells me there's a lot more to him than that."

Rhona's eyes lit at the mention of the man's name. "Well, we're a new thing, you know. In relative terms anyway. He had a wife but she died in childbirth. One of the rare ways a Fae can die other than an accident, being murdered or of very old age. For a thousand years he closed himself off to women. He's loosened up in the last three hundred years or so. Certainly long enough to have brought his best work to my bed of late."

"How terrible for him. The child?"

"She's a weaver. A fine artist and a lovely girl. He has family to help. A lovely thing, Haley. We're here for you too, when you look around you'll see us. We're not all as annoying as Aideen."

Haley laughed and turned her head as she caught sight of

Conall standing in the doorway, his arm around a man who mirrored him except the other man's hair was a tawny blond instead of Conall's deep night.

He looked sheepish a moment until she smiled at him and he relaxed.

"Ah, I see Riordan is returned. My two favorite cousins." Rhona waved and jumped down to hug Riordan while Conall made his way to Haley.

"I'm sorry I acted like an ass. My father chewed me a new one as did Rhona, my mother and half the *brugh*. Even Riordan and he doesn't even know you." Conall brushed his mouth over hers and she hugged him.

"And this lovely redhead must be Haley. Too pretty to be snagged by my idiot brother but the bond is mysterious that way." He grinned. "I hear you saved his soul. Thank you for bringing him back to us."

Haley looked around Conall's body to see Riordan macCormac looking her over through eyes so pale green they were nearly yellow.

He shoved Conall aside and scooped Haley up in a hug.

"Ho there, put my wife down now or I'll have to sever your dangly bits."

Conall watched Haley with his cousin and brother and smiled. He'd been so pissed off last night, stung that she'd refused to go to dinner, but it wasn't until she'd given him space he realized she needed some herself, and he felt even worse.

Seeing Riordan while Conall had been walking about looking for Haley had made the afternoon a million times better and hearing news Haley was at the pub put him back on track.

But when she'd smiled at him, he knew everything would be fine and all was forgiven.

"I'd steal your redheaded little Irish queen in half a second if I could. But Mum'd have my arse so I suppose I'll have to keep my charms to myself. Or," he winked at Haley, "confined to all women who you aren't married to."

They grabbed a booth and visited for long hours and many pints.

"I must go and get some sleep. I have a Foundation meeting tomorrow and then tea with my grandmother." Haley stood.

Anger rose in Conall's gut but he tamped it down, especially after Riordan kicked his shin under the table.

"That's going to leave a mark," he mumbled to his brother as they all headed toward the doors.

"Good. Remember what I told you. Your woman is fierce. You cannot cage her or you'll lose her. She needs to honor her family as you honor yours."

"She's also reckless and I worry I'll lose her if Ninane gets it into her head to harm her."

"I can hear you both you know. *She's* also not hard of hearing," Haley called back over her shoulder, amusing his brother to no end.

"Just wait, Riordan. Your time will come when you meet your match." But Conall grinned as he said it.

Chapter Eleven

Conall was truly going to kill her if something happened to her while she was out and about.

Haley tried not to glance over her shoulder again but she felt it nonetheless. All day long she'd felt as if someone was following her. She knew it was silly and part of her wanted to kick Conall's butt for putting the idea in her head to start with.

Conall wasn't with her because he'd had to attend Aoife for something. A justice emergency—Haley had teased him. But when the queen called, you attended. And it wasn't as if Haley had an armed escort before she met Conall. And okay, fine, she did admit she hadn't had a crazed Fae bitch on some sort of mission to kill her on her back then either. But still. She couldn't let all this paranoia rule her life. She'd be careful but not so careful she lived in fear every moment.

Anyway, it was Haley who trained as a warrior. Granted, Conall's magic was a great deal stronger than hers, but she could handle herself in a scuffle and sift out of there if need be.

She'd had her meeting at the Foundation, had tea with her gran and they'd both sifted to have a light meal with her parents but it was getting late and Haley had used the scrying bowl to let Conall know she was going to grab some groceries for her parents at the corner bodega before heading home. Her gran would stay the week with her parents before heading back to Ireland and Haley hoped her mother had a secret stash of liquor somewhere to help her get through the days. The two women were like oil and water.

Haley laughed as she thought of how her gran had already reorganized the spices in the cabinet and of her mother's look of outrage when she'd discovered it.

Her laugh strangled in her throat as she felt the tingle of magic and ducked as instinct drove her to, the bag holding the groceries flying to the pavement.

Good thing as a bolt of energy flew right where her head would have been. She tucked her legs and rolled up into a crouch. She took a risk, using her magic in public and her blade filled her right hand. Panic threatened to steal her ability to think straight and focus. Her attacker got a quick, hard jab to her chin before she was able to rein in her fear and concentrate.

Feinting to the left, she reached out, slicing through the arm of her attacker, bringing a howl of pain and the metallic scent of spilled blood. He sprang back, kicking her solidly in the ribs, knocking the air from her and following with a baton to her back, right to her kidneys. An explosion of pain shot through her side, narrowing her vision for long moments.

He hit her again and another time once more and she knew a second man waited just outside her reach. She wouldn't make it if she didn't fall back on the training she'd received from Aoife over the last months. If she didn't handle this now, her family would be in jeopardy.

On his next pass, she'd gathered herself enough to dodge, catching his leg and wrenching it to push him off his feet. Within moments he was on her again but she swept her leg out and knocked him off his feet and gave him a solid boot to the temple and he stayed down.

She needed to sift but they were two blocks from her parents' house. What if she left and the attackers knew and went straight to them? Haley couldn't take the chance, she didn't want to risk them.

A violent punch to the face pushed the breath out of her as she stumbled back to get her balance. The force of the punch had split her lip and eyebrow. Blood stung as it ran into her eye. A roll of her wrist and a lunge toward the second man brought the edge of her blade into contact with him. Triumph brought a new spurt of energy when she heard a hiss of pain.

A set of strong arms locked around her middle and her magic dampened. A human using cold iron. Fuck.

But she didn't need magic to fight. She drove her head back and heard the crack of his nose as she saw stars.

"Don't let her get away!"

Haley looked and saw the curvaceous pale blonde just ahead. Ninane the psycho, she guessed.

Haley twisted as the man holding her gurgled and she got enough leverage to poke him hard in the throat. When he dropped her, she rocked back and gave him a hard kick right to the balls and he crumpled with a wet-sounding wheeze.

Haley spun to face the other woman, pulling as much magic into herself as she could. "Let me guess, you're Ninane. The bitch. Come on then, let's do this so I can get a little payback for what you put my husband through."

Brave words but Haley was pissed. So pissed she gave the asshole another kick in the junk and a follow up shot to the kidneys. He wouldn't be getting up any time soon.

"You'll pay for this, human whore. I promise you that."

Haley jumped to the concrete as magic singed past her head. Okay, this was stupid and she was injured, exhausted and in way over her head. Time to fall back. She sifted but not to her parents' house. To her old high school first and then back to her parents'. She didn't want Ninane to be able to trace her.

Haley hurried into the living room on a limp. "Gran, get them out of here. Ninane attacked me and tried to kidnap me. I have to tell Conall, get them looking for her. In fact, new plan, you all come back with me," Haley ordered, knowing she must have looked a sight with blood all over her, arm clutched at her side.

Thank goodness her gran saw the seriousness and didn't even question her. She stood up and gathered Haley's parents. "We'll sift to my house. It's thoroughly warded and no one but those my magic is keyed to can enter. You go on right now. Conall needs to know and you'll need a healer."

Her father kissed her cheek, looking livid when he caught sight of the blooming bruise on her cheek from the big beefy human's punch. "Don't argue with your grandmother. Go. Now. Check in as soon as you can."

Haley made them sift first and then followed, using a back entry to the *sithein* rather than the front one in case Ninane was waiting. She reached the back gates before she crumpled and called out the guard's name.

Conall had been polishing off one last pint when he heard the shouting in the square. Riordan, his father and Mal all stood and rushed out with him.

One of the guards from the rear gate ran toward him after jumping off his horse. "Conall, thank the Lady you're here. It's your Haley, she's been hurt. We've taken her home. A healer is on the way."

Adrenaline filled him as he headed for home at a full run,

the pounding steps of his brother, father and friend behind him. When he burst through their door, Aoife was there and several guards stood at attention.

Aoife's strong hands caught his shoulders. "She's upstairs, Conall. She's all right. I give you my word. The doctor is with her now. Take a deep breath before you see her. I know you're upset but she doesn't need you to take that out on her." His aunt looked at him sternly and he let out the breath he'd been holding.

"Do we know what happened?" His hands shook and his father squeezed his shoulder briefly.

"Ninane tried to kidnap her. She had men with her, they assaulted Haley, beat her. But she got here on her own steam, she's banged up but she'll be all right. Hear that, Conall. I've sent some of my guards out to investigate the scene and report back and I've also sent people to check on Maeve and Haley's parents, who're with her. They've sifted to Maeve's home for the time being. I've offered them a home here or guards if they wish to stay out."

"I've got to go to her." He needed to see with his own eyes, to touch her and know she was all right. Aoife nodded and Conall ran upstairs, only barely resisting the urge to kick down the bedroom door to get to her.

Nothing could have prepared him for the sight of Haley, her eye half swollen shut, bruise livid over her cheek, blood in her hair and on her skin and salve on her lip and eyebrow.

"Goddess..." He stumbled, moving to her, trying to rein in his urgency to touch her, knowing he needed to be gentle but feeling anything but.

The doctor held her hand out to Conall to stay him and led him to the bed where he sat, just barely touching her but enough to calm him. Haley reached out, placing her hand in

125

his.

"She's going to be fine. A black eye as you can see. Split her lip and her eyebrow. The man must have been monstrously large to have a fist so big. Her ribs are sore, one is broken so I've got her all taped up. No internal bleeding and she's already beginning to heal. Some bruising around her kidneys. Don't be alarmed if there's a bit of blood in your urine, Haley. Torn tendons in her shoulder, it was dislocated but I've remedied that. Your missus wasn't too very fond of me at that moment, I must say."

Haley laughed and then coughed as she winced in pain.

"And laughing will hurt for a while in case you hadn't noticed. Sleep, Haley. Your system will do the rest. You'll have that rib back in tip top shape by the time you wake up and the bruise should ease overnight as well. The powder I gave you to drink should help you sleep. If you need me, you know where I am."

Conall walked the doctor to the door of the bedroom and turned back to Haley. Tears ran down her face and he held back his own as he moved to gently enfold her.

"Oh, goddess, thank you for letting my woman be all right," Conall murmured into Haley's hair. "I love you, Haley, but I'm going to kick your pretty little Irish ass if you even so much as think about leaving the *sithein* until we find Ninane."

She nodded against him slowly. "I love you too. I need to contact my family. They're at my gran's. I have to know they're all right."

"Lay down and rest. I'll have Riordan speak with Aoife. She sent some guards to check and then I will be back. I want to hear every detail of what happened."

Conall went out to the landing and saw his brother had been waiting, his face serious.

"Is she all right?"

Conall nodded with a sigh. "She's not a pretty sight just now, Ninane will pay as will the men who marked her face and broke her rib. Check and see how her family is, please. Haley is worried and I know she won't rest until she knows."

"Mother is downstairs, she wants to come up. Da made her stay until you came out. What do you say?" Riordan waited for his answer and Conall was thankful his older brother had returned. Glad to have the support and backup.

"She can come up for a bit. She'll not overtax Haley and Haley will need a bit of mothering I'd wager. Not Aideen though. I'm afraid my wife is still miffed with our little sister." Conall kept his voice low and Riordan laughed.

"Be right back then."

Conall had just settled in next to Haley when his mother came in, followed by Haley's own mother, father and grandmother.

"I've brought you something I thought might make you feel better, sweetheart." Dana smiled but Conall caught the wince when his mother took in the battered face.

Haley's mother rushed to her, falling to her knees next to the bed. Riordan got chairs for everyone and Aoife and Cormac joined them when Haley gave the complete story of what had happened.

He was sure steam poured from his ears when she'd finished, just thinking about what Ninane could have done to Haley with her magic. Why the hell had she gone grocery shopping in the first place? She could have just conjured the food herself. He shoved his need to demand she admit how stupid she'd been far away. She wanted to take care of her parents just as he did. She'd been human for twenty-five years so it wasn't as if she'd automatically resort to what Fae did

127

anyway. And her mother's discomfort with magic and Haley's new status as a Faerie would have complicated matters. He wanted to punch something.

That urge came back in force when her family, well really her mother, agreed to stay for a day or two, until they'd ascertained if it was safe or not for them to leave. Haley had tried to argue they remain in the *brugh* for at least a few weeks but Conall could see how uncomfortable Haley's mother was and he doubted that would happen. He felt bad for it, it was almost as if her mother rejected part of her by showing such intense discomfort with the Fae and magic but he said nothing to Haley about it.

Finally, she kept nodding off and Maeve shooed everyone out before pressing a gentle kiss on Haley's forehead and leaving as well. They'd stay in one of the guest cottages near Aoife's estate and promised to see Haley in the morning.

After she'd finally dropped off into a deep sleep, Conall had walked through the house, re-checking the wards his aunt and mother had re-done with Maeve's magic woven in. Guards were posted outside and his brother sat on the couch, flipping through a book.

They'd spoken in hushed tones for some time, planning, plotting but mainly letting Conall unload his fear, his anger, his guilt and shame that he hadn't been there when Haley needed him most.

His father came in and sent Riordan to bed, taking over and sending Conall up to Haley's side with a hug and an admonition not to let this drive a wedge between the two of them.

The moon streamed in through the window, dusting her with silver and he tried to get hold of his racing heart. But *she* was his heart and he could have lost her. He hadn't been with her and because of that she could have died.

The pain of what might have been sliced through him, nearly suffocating him with angst and dread. Yes, he'd been concerned about Ninane but he'd mostly bought into Haley's assurances that he was overreacting. He hadn't been and Ninane could have stolen his heart from him as well as his soul.

Her eyes fluttered open and she stared at him for long moments. "Are you mad at me?"

He couldn't contain the raw sound bubbling up from his gut as he moved to their bed and slid in beside her. As gently as he could, he snuggled her against him.

"I love you, Haley. I'm not mad at you. You wanted to see your parents. You...I should have been there. I'm sorry. Are you mad at me?"

She sobbed as she shook her head. "I was so afraid, Conall. I was afraid I'd die and never see you again. Never be able to tell you how much finding you meant to me, how much I love you. I'm not mad at you. Why would you think that?"

Her admission of fear, the woman who was so big she took up every corner of any room she entered, shattered him. He kissed her gently, tasting her fear, her pain and anguish and tucked her back against his body.

"I've got you, Irish witch. I've got you and nothing will happen to you, I vow it. Now go to sleep and let your body heal."

Chapter Twelve

Haley's parents had gone back to San Francisco several days after the attack. She'd been disappointed her mother had been so uncomfortable in the *brugh* that she'd chosen to leave and face any possible danger, but as her gran had said, Haley couldn't change her mother's mind so she had to let it go. It was difficult not to take that personally but she'd do her best.

Maeve had stayed on another week, getting to know Conall's family and their tribe more. She'd even been at the ceremony where Haley had taken on her tribal marking.

Within days of the attack, Haley was back, training with Aoife and Cormac. Riordan had joined them, bringing firearms into the program. Where Rhona had become her best-girlfriend, Riordan had become the brother she never had. He was one of the few people Conall was totally open and himself with and Haley loved to see the relationship between the two brothers. She also thought it was dead sexy he'd been in the British Special Forces for twenty years before moving to the United States and training as an Army Ranger. Essentially, he'd spent decades honing himself as a highly trained super soldier and he'd been trying to convince Aoife of the need to have a Fae version of the Special Forces.

The more Haley learned about Fae history, the more she agreed with her brother-in-law's opinion. There were those Fae,

Fae referred to as dark or rogue Fae, who were opposed to the line of separation from humanity. They didn't care about sharing the universe with those less powerful. They didn't think it was necessary to share at all when they could simply control whatever they wanted to, including other Fae tribes who were considered weaker.

The tribe Ninane had been sheltered by was one of those considered the most dangerous. Twice they'd attempted to overthrow the *Daoine* and had been pushed back. A treaty bound by Aoife's promise was all that stood between a new war. They didn't have enough proof their king, Dugan, had been involved with Ninane's plan and attack on Conall to consider his part of the treaty broken.

Haley continued her work with the archives but also began to work with Cormac and Riordan with the Queen's Guard. Of course that made Conall crazy but at least she was inside the *brugh* all the time and with his father and brother so he kept his complaints to a minimum.

They'd kept a close eye on the *sithein* and there hadn't been any further sightings of Ninane in the month following the attack but they still did not relax.

Conall watched the graceful way Haley took the steep path to their door. He loved the way she moved, sensual and lithe. Her hair was bound back in a long braid and it swung from side to side like a metronome.

He met her at the door, taking her mouth for a kiss before she could even say hello. Every time he left her for the day and she came back to him later, safely, the relief rushing through him was enough to knock him off his feet and sweep her into bed.

If they even made it to bed.

Mouth still on hers, tasting her, drinking her in, he caressed every part of her he could reach, yanking and ripping as he went, needing to touch her bare skin.

She writhed against him, suckling his tongue, her fingers pulling at the waist of his jeans to open them.

They could have used magic and sometimes he did, not being able to wait long enough to do it by hand, but the sort of urgent, desperate symphony of movement to get the other naked enough for sex appealed to him more than the instant naked of magically removing her clothes.

She shoved him back and fell to her knees as he bumped into the wall just behind him. She grabbed the belt loops of his jeans and pulled hard, exposing his cock as the denim held him in place, locking around his ankles.

Sensation swam through his senses as he watched down the line of his body when she took his cock in her hands. A sound of anticipation, unbidden, slipped from him as she licked her lips before taking him into her mouth. His breath exploded from him at the sensation of her tongue swirling around the crown.

She took her time, bringing a bit more of him into her each time she pressed forward. The heated wet of her mouth, followed by the cool air as she pulled back. Over and over, a little more into her. A dig of the tip of her tongue into the spot right below the head, a gentle scoring of his balls with her nails, she brought him more pleasure by the moment and he could do little more than stay afloat as he tried not to drown in her.

He was grateful the wall behind him took his weight or the things she did with her mouth would have buckled his knees.

When she pulled off with a gentle popping sound, her lips were swollen and wet. His heart beat so fast he felt dizzy.

"I love sucking your cock, Conall. I love how powerful it

makes me feel to give you so much pleasure. I love the way you taste. I love how naughty I feel when your cock is in my mouth."

Blinkblinkblink. For a long moment he was robbed of speech. She was so beautiful there on her knees, her eyes glazed with passion, lips swollen from his cock. Her words meant only for him.

"Lady, you're amazing. I love you, Haley. You undo me."

One corner of her mouth quirked up and she gripped the base of him before swallowing him as deeply as she could over and over. He closed his eyes and just felt.

It wasn't too long before climax sent him hot down her throat and then to his knees, dragging her with him as they laughed together.

Still tangled in his jeans, he'd been about to resort to magic, three fingers deep inside her pussy when someone knocked on the door just a few feet away.

They froze, hoping whoever it was would go away.

Haley lay there, Conall's fingers inside her and prayed he wouldn't say a word.

"Conall! It's Aideen. I know you're home. Come on and open up. I thought you and Haley might like to come to dinner. Riordan is here with me too and Brenna will meet us at the pub in a few minutes."

Haley ground her teeth and shoved Conall's hand out of her panties. Nothing like Aideen's voice to splash cold water all over her libido.

"I wasn't done," he whispered.

"I am. Go on, get up and answer the door." Haley sat up and with some quick magic, got herself changed and back in order.

"We don't have to do anything with them. I wanted to spend tonight just you and me." He winked and she would have relented had Aideen not pounded on the door again.

"She knows what we're doing and she doesn't care. Open the fucking door, I'm no longer in the mood." Haley stood, not bothering to lower her voice.

"You're too hard on her," he said quietly as he moved to the door to open it.

"And you're not hard enough. I'm not having this discussion again. I'd not go at all but you'll pout and I'll have to hear about how *well-meaning* she is for days and I don't want to be mad at you."

He sighed and opened the door. Haley caught Riordan's eye as he'd been pulling Aideen away from the door and he shrugged apologetically.

"Oh, did I interrupt?" Aideen giggled and Haley only barely held back a sneer.

"Dinner you say? Sure, let's go." Conall smiled at Aideen and turned back to Haley who rolled her eyes.

"Yes, heaven forbid we not jump right to it," she said quietly as she avoided his hand and went outside, quickly moving past her sister-in-law.

Aideen was such a pain in her ass. Why couldn't it be like in a romance when all the women in the man's family loved and got along with the heroine? Dana was lovely, Brenna, Conall's other sister was wonderful and Haley adored her. The various female cousins like Rhona were fun and friendly and she'd made friends with them all. But Aideen was like that girl at church camp who told on everyone who smuggled in candy bars or said a naughty word. The worst thing was how Riordan and Conall coddled her. The woman was two thousand years old! It wasn't like she was an infant or anything.

So they walked to the pub and Conall put his arm around her shoulders. She loved the way he felt like that, against her, his warmth seeping into her body, the scent of him wrapping around her senses.

At the same time, her captivity in the *brugh* wore on her nearly as bad as Aideen had and it bristled. Agitated anew, she pulled away and Riordan caught the moment of discord as he opened the door for everyone.

"Haley, can I speak to you a moment? I meant to tell you earlier when we were at the firing range but I forgot." Riordan gave her the same charming guy smile Conall used and it jumped right on her nerves.

"No." She pushed past and went into the pub.

She scooted into the booth next to Brenna and her husband Patrick, giving them both a kiss on the cheek. Rhona caught her attention and rolled her eyes discreetly.

Conall sat beside her, trapping her while Riordan and Aideen slid in across from them. Haley gave in and relaxed against Conall's side as he twirled a strand of her hair around a fingertip while they talked and ate.

It wasn't until the third pint and after the conclusion of a meal consisting of some very tasty shepherd's pie that things took a turn.

"You know, Haley, I could have told you training like a man would make you touchy. It's not very flattering," Aideen said.

Haley closed her eyes a moment and felt Conall tense up.

"Aideen, Haley is quite good at combat and training. I happen to think it's very flattering." Conall squeezed the arm around Haley's shoulder.

"What I mean is, it seems to make her even moodier than usual. She doesn't seem very happy here and I think it's because she's not even bothering to try and fit in. It's like how she kept on leaving here even though it made you worry and put her in danger. I'm just saying it's not very flattering when she disrespects her husband so much. And his family."

"And on that note, I'll say goodnight. I'm going to get up and leave this table right now before I say what I'm really thinking." Haley shoved at Conall but he wouldn't move.

"No one needs to leave. Aideen, you're out of line. I know you're worried about me and I know you care, but Haley is my wife and she doesn't disrespect me at all. You two need to make amends. Get to know each other." Conall gave that reasonable-dude smile and Haley wanted to throw her beer in his face.

"I've tried, Conall, and she's always like this. I came to your home tonight to invite you to dinner and this is how she acts!" Aideen pouted.

Brenna shushed her sister and Rhona clucked. Both women glared at Aideen.

"Conall, this is your last warning. If you do not let me out of this booth right now, I will not hold back any longer," Haley said in a low voice.

"Haley, can't you give it a try?"

"Try? Like, give up my life outside this *sithein* and live here? Give up my position on a foundation I worked years of my life to be appointed to? Give up seeing my family on a regular basis? Give up my friends and my apartment, give up my cell phone, baseball, dance clubs? No TIVO, no movies at the Cineplex, no takeout Chinese. No cars! Come here, to another world and make every effort to be part of your life and family? Take more than anyone's normal share of bullshit from your nosy-assed, busy-body, passive-aggressive sister while you say *nothing* to back me up until she openly insults me, once again? Try like that?"

"She's trying, Haley. You take things the wrong way," Riordan said. "You just don't know her."

"I don't get you people. And I don't want to. In my family, if someone pulled this crap, they'd get called on it."

"Your mother couldn't stand to be here for longer than a day. She can't accept your Fae blood! Some family you have," Aideen said furiously.

"Off sides!" Conall stood up and Haley pushed past him but he caught her arm.

"Let me go, now!" If he didn't, she was going to throw down with her sister-in-law.

"Not yet, Haley. Aideen, you owe Haley an apology and right now." Conall's voice was stern and Aideen's bottom lip trembled.

"I'm sorry. I didn't mean it."

Haley would not give any of them a single tear. She made her voice as flat as possible. "Yes you did. Don't you think I know my mother left here because she can't deal with my magic and who I am? Do you have any idea how much that hurts? You used it to hurt me on purpose and I don't give a rat's ass if your siblings want to remain blind to it or not. You're a bitter, petty, small person, Aideen. Hateful and spiteful. I'm done." She shrugged off Conall's hand and stormed out.

"Haley!" Conall chased her but she kept walking until he caught up with her in their front garden.

"I'm sorry. Haley, stop. I'm sorry she said that. It was uncalled for and I would never have you hurt that way. Not by anyone, least of all my own sister." His voice softened as he looked into her face.

"I'm never going to the pub with her again. Never going to her house for dinner. Not going to sit and soak in the springs with her either. She is not welcome in our home if I am there."

He sighed and pulled her to him. "If that's what you want, Haley. I respect your wishes. I wish you could see she's not as bad as you think. Yes, what she said was wrong and yes, she said it to hurt you. But she's threatened by you. Everyone loves you. She feels like you've usurped her spot."

"I don't want you trying to make me feel sorry for her, Conall. She's not a child. You keep treating her that way so she keeps on doing it. But she's two thousand years old. I swear to you, if you or anyone else makes an apology for her behavior or tells me I misunderstand poor little Aideen I will leave here. I'm not joking. Because if I don't leave, I'd knock the person speaking on their ass."

He sighed and she pushed him off. "I love you, Haley. But I love my family too and I want you to love them. They love you."

"I'm going inside. I won't be made to be the villain of this piece. If that's your plan, run on over to Aideen's now so you can sob in her skirts. I don't have the energy."

"Oi!" Haley turned from Conall to see Rhona standing at the gate below holding a bag. "I've got sweets and a few bottles here. As it appears you're not having make-up sex, you want to come to my house to cool down a while?"

Haley went down the steps and hugged the other woman tight. "Thank you. But I'm going to steam, take a bath and go to bed. I'll see you tomorrow at the archives."

"Aideen is a right git. Brenna is chewing her out right now. When Dana hears, well, I wouldn't want to be Aideen. You going to be all right? Haley, your mother...well it's not about you. You get that don't you? She doesn't know how to connect with the part of you that's made her totally different from your dad all their time together and now you forever. She's a woman of science. Of ration and reason and this place is just too much

for her to try and fit into her head."

"I promised myself I wouldn't cry," Haley sniffled, wiping her face on her sleeve.

She felt Conall's alarm as she cried. He moved toward them but Rhona held a hand out to stay him.

"You go on then. Get some rest. I love you. You're a dear friend and so very welcome in this *brugh*. I'll see you tomorrow." Rhona kissed her cheek and with a tight hug, she was gone.

Haley stood, watching her go until she'd moved out of sight. With a sigh, she turned and nearly rammed into Conall, who'd been standing only a few feet away.

"I'm going inside."

"Haley, I hate when you're upset. Please, let's talk this out."

"Conall, I'm going to take a long, hot bath. Alone. I will eat too much chocolate and masturbate. Alone. And then I will go to sleep. I don't want to talk about your sister. I don't want to talk about how I misjudge her. I don't want to hear a word defending her or I swear to you I will head for the gates and sift to my grandmother's house. I love you." She kissed him before he could argue and jogged around him and into the house.

He watched her leave, not knowing what to do. He loved his wife so very much and he could see how upset she was. And rightfully so. Aideen had really mucked things up with her comments at the pub. She'd wounded Haley deeply.

He wasn't used to domestic fights. He and Haley had plenty of heat between them. Little tiffs here and there but almost always about her safety and his need to protect her. After the attack the month before, she'd respected his wishes and had stayed home even though he knew she chafed to see her family. Since then, their only disagreements had been about who got to be on top and of course, Aideen.

He just wished Haley understood Aideen better. Aideen was jealous and worried and she struck out at Haley because she wasn't Haley. Despite her being two thousand years old, emotionally, Aideen was very young.

"Good Lord and Lady, boy! What are you doing out here? Did your ladywife toss your butt out into the lane then?"

Conall turned to see his brother standing at the gate. "Riordan, don't you speak ill of Haley, she's had a very unpleasant day."

His frown slid away, replaced by a grin. "I wasn't speaking ill of my sister-in-law. I quite like your Haley. If she wasn't yours, I'd steal her in half the blink of an eye. No, I was speaking ill of you and me and our ninny of a sister. I wanted to come by and offer my apology to your fair maid."

"Stop talking like Robin Hood. She's pissed off at me. She cried. Fuck. Then she told me she was going for a bath, some chocolate and a wank and to leave her alone."

Riordan's eyebrows shot up. "I believe that's one of those TMI moments, brother. I really don't want to think about your wife all slick and wet, her hand sliding down her body..."

"Hey!" Conall shoved Riordan's shoulder to shut him up. "Stop that."

"You're the one who started it." Riordan laughed. "If you've got that pretty redhead inside, um, getting busy in your bathroom, what are you doing out here instead of groveling in there?"

"You've got a point. Get out of here." Conall ran up the steps and into their house. He locked up, turned out the lights and headed toward the bathroom where he heard the water running.

"Haley?" He tapped on the door.

He heard her groan as she stepped into the bath and his entire body tightened. He remembered how beautiful she'd been earlier after she'd sucked his cock, the way her lips had looked, her eyes holding only him. And he'd chosen to go to dinner instead of that? He was an idiot.

"Haley, honey, I'm coming in." Thankfully, she hadn't locked the door and he entered the bath and her scent hit him like a fist.

"I told you I wanted to be left alone," she mumbled drowsily. She didn't even bother to open her eyes as she floated lazily in the water. A glass of wine sat perched on the edge of the tub next to a gold box of Godiva chocolates. She was an able hand with her magic. It made him smile even though he felt like an idiot.

"I know what you said. Haley, I'm sorry." He got rid of his clothes and sank into the water but didn't crowd her just at the moment. "You were right. I should have taken your side and more strongly from the start. You're my wife. My mate, and I wasn't there when you needed me. Can you forgive me?"

She cracked an eye open and then the other. "Conall, why are you here? Really?"

He sensed she needed total honesty from him and it wasn't the time to prevaricate or hold back. He took a deep breath and reached inside himself and hoped he could put it as plainly as he felt.

"I'm here because I hate the thought of you unhappy or feeling alone. Almost as much as I hate my contributing to it. I should make you feel like my family. I should make you comfortable and safe and welcome. And I didn't when I needed to most. I didn't listen the way I should have. You're mine to cherish, Haley, and I didn't. Your heart is my most precious

141

possession."

She sat up fully and he tried very hard not to look at the way the water cascaded down her body.

"I'm sorry. I know it's two words and they don't mean much after the way you were treated tonight and, well, for some time by my sister and me too. But all I can do is say it, mean it and promise you I'll work hard to make sure it doesn't happen again."

He moved closer to her, reaching out to trace a fingertip along her jawline. "I don't want to lose you. I love you."

"I love you too. And I love your family, even Aideen. But right now she's out of line and it's unacceptable. I don't want to hear excuses for her. I don't want to be the bigger person over this, damn it. She took something only a family member would know and used it to hurt me. That's not all right. It's not just a silly mistake. She did it on purpose. I'm not saying it makes her as evil as Ninane, but it makes her accountable. And she will be or things will never be all right between her and me."

Conall nodded. Put that way, Haley was entirely reasonable and entirely correct. "However you want to handle it, I'll back you up."

"All right. You're forgiven." She kissed him quickly and leaned back, taking a sip of her wine and choosing a chocolate she popped into her mouth.

"Haley?"

"Hmm?"

"About that masturbation comment..."

She smiled but her eyes remained closed. "What about it? I can wait until you're done in here."

"You're deviling me." He moved through the water and lay against her, floating. "Show me."

"No. I'm feeling lazy now. I don't feel like entertaining you."

"You're being very uncooperative." He nuzzled her ear, feeling her shiver against him.

"Suckit. I'm not feeling cooperative."

He laughed. "Suckit? You've got a graduate degree and that's what you tell me?"

"Sometimes, Conall, simple is best." She opened her eyes and arched a single brow at him.

Still laughing, he scrambled to his feet, bringing her with him. Using his magic to dry them off, he went into their bedroom and tossed her on the bed.

"What are you doing?"

He loved the sound of her laughter, loved it when she looked at him with affection like the way she did just then.

"Why, darling Irish witch, I'm getting ready to suck it."

"Oh! Well then." She spread her thighs. "Don't let me stop you."

And then his mouth was on her, warm and wet, his tongue sliding against her in all her favorite places. Knowing just where she liked it and how rough.

He took his time, maddeningly slow as he licked around her clit but never actually touched it. He dipped his tongue deep into her, curling it up and fluttering it as she clenched around him.

Back out, lapping at her. A heated flush stole up her body. Every inch of her skin tingled as the air caressed her. It wasn't Conall using his magic, it was the way he made her feel.

Her nipples throbbed in time with her pulse and he did something wicked with his fingers against her gate as he finally breathed a small touch over her clit.

143

He latched his mouth around her clit and sucked, not too hard, not too soft, but in and out, bringing the edge of his teeth against the sensitive flesh over and over as he thrust his fingers into her.

Electric pleasure arced up her spine as it bowed and she came hard with blinding intensity.

When she came back to herself, he lay on her thigh, looking up at her with a smug smile, licking his lips slowly.

"That was some of your best work." Her words were desire thick.

"Well, that was just the lunch hour. I'm ready to get back to it."

Chapter Thirteen

"Samhain is coming up in a week, Conall. I promised my grandmother's people I'd come and see them for it. They want to throw a wedding banquet for us. And I haven't seen my parents in five months. I miss them. I miss my grandmother." Haley sat up in bed, the sheet falling down enough to expose a nipple he'd just held between his teeth a few minutes before.

Conall exhaled sharply and tried to rein in his impatience. "She's still out there. You promised you'd stay here until we dealt with her." He reached for her to drag her back but she snorted and slapped his hand away.

"I've lived in this *brugh* for nine months under a constant threat. I've missed my mom's birthday and the groundbreaking ceremonies for the new labs for the Foundation. I can't stay in these eight square miles forever. I'll go insane. I want to go to the beach. I want to go skiing. I want to go shopping and watch the A's play a game. I've been here without complaint for months but it has to end at some point."

"It's been so peaceful for the last four months. After that initial first month with Aideen and all, that is. I brought in movies so we could see them, didn't I? You have your girls' nights with your friends here now. No fights between us. You've been training and my father and brother have stolen you from the archives. You seemed happy. What's changed?"

She leaned down and kissed him. "I am happy. Don't be daft. That doesn't mean I don't miss my mom and dad. Stop thinking about this like it's either/or. It's not that way. But I want my whole life. I'm not asking to leave every day. You can come with me, or send Riordan with me. We can sift right to my grandmother's house or even to her tribe's land up north. We'll be safe there. I won't be stupid. I promise. Plus, dude, I'm very handy with a weapon these days. Just ask Aoife."

"No, Haley. You promised and I'm not risking you. I could have lost you and that won't happen again. It won't be forever and your family is always welcome here." Her damned mother was a pain in the ass with her skittishness about the *sithein*. It hurt Haley and it put her in danger that they wouldn't come visit and she'd have to go there.

"My promise didn't mean forever." She got out of bed and stormed into the bathroom.

He sensed her growing impatience, especially as Samhain approached and their promised visit with the Traveling Folk was right around the corner. He didn't blame her. He chafed at being kept in the *sithein* as well and all his family and friends were there. His human family hadn't really missed him as he'd had a strained relationship with them before anyway.

They hadn't left the *sithein* in five months. She'd been pretty patient and he'd known it would end soon enough. She wasn't one to sit around at all. But he didn't care. She promised to stay there until they'd dealt with Ninane and that was all there was to it. He would not risk her.

Haley trained with such ferocity Aoife stopped her and laughed. "Darling, what is going on with you? Come and take a ride with me." Aoife looked over at Cormac who scowled. "Oh pish posh! I'll keep within the inner gates and you can come too. The girl has been in the confines of the *brugh* for months now without a break. She needs to get out or she's going to hack off one of my limbs."

Haley blushed. "I'm sorry. Yes, I'd love to and yes, the house arrest is driving me crazy."

They went on their ride and Haley did feel a lot better after racing Dulce and feeling the wind in her hair and the power of her horse beneath her.

Back in the stables while they fed and watered the horses, Riordan took over when Aoife went back to do her queen-type stuff.

"I know you're frustrated, Haley. But Conall is worried. Scared. He nearly lost you when Ninane attacked before. You have to hold on. We're looking for Ninane." Riordan walked along with her as they headed back to town.

She sighed. "Riordan, imagine if you couldn't see your family when you were used to seeing them them all the time, spoke to them on the phone at least three times a week. We know where Ninane is. She's below and we can't get in there without breaking the treaty. So it's an impasse. How long will this go on? She's lying low and I'm in here. Samhain is two days away. I'm strong. You're strong. You could come with us and with you there, Conall wouldn't have to worry as much. Just from the gates straight to the tribe's lands. Which are safe and you know it."

"Haley, don't you flutter those lashes at me. It doesn't work. I'll talk to Conall on your behalf and see what he says. Okay?"

Didn't work, her ass. Putty, big, tough Riordan macCormac was a big giant ball of goo. Well, when he wasn't being all super soldier and stuff.

"Thank you." She tiptoed up and kissed his cheek quickly and he snorted.

"Yes well, tonight is big family dinner night. Brenna's birthday. You can show your appreciation by coming with Conall. Please."

She and Aideen had come to an uneasy peace but there was no way she'd snub Brenna or the rest of Conall's family for a celebration.

"Of course. I've come to family events before this and not torn anyone's head off." She did have to give Conall credit, he solidly backed her up and Aideen had ceased with the comments. It also helped that Dana sent Aideen a scowl any time it looked as if she was going to say anything.

"Go on then, I'll watch until you get to the door." Riordan opened the gate and she went in, stopping to pick some flowers on her way.

Despite her ire at not being able to leave, she loved this place. Loved her home with Conall. Often, they'd sit out on the deck outside their bedroom in the evenings, the scent of the flowers wafting on the breeze.

Conall was a thousand times the man she ever dreamed she'd fall in love with. He was funny and sexy, intelligent and compassionate. Every day there was another reason she loved him. It'd been nine months since they'd been together that first time, nearly a year and a half since she'd met him and even when she was so mad at him she wanted to slam a door, her love for him was never in doubt.

Sometimes she went to the halls of justice near the town center to watch him work. His voice solemn as he argued a case or sent down a judgment, she listened to him, appreciated his intelligence and sense of justice and duty.

She knew why he wanted her to stay within the safest zone of the *brugh*. She understood he wanted her safe and she wanted that too. But she wouldn't let Ninane keep her prisoner in her own damned home. And she wouldn't let Ninane stop her from having a relationship with her family either. She'd kept Conall away from his for a thousand years. Haley didn't have that time, her parents were mortal and she didn't want to give that kind of power to the other woman either. Ninane had done enough damage.

"Hello, Irish witch. You look deep in thought."

Tipping her head up, she drank in the sight of Conall on the porch, wearing a low slung pair of jeans, a snug T-shirt. His hair was loose, hanging to his waist. Clear blue eyes took her in.

"I was thinking about how sexy you were when you did your job." She smiled and took his hand, allowing him to pull her into the house.

"Really now?" He leaned down and kissed her slow and deep, taking his time and leaving her breathless.

"Wow. You're so good at that."

"I've had a wee bit of practice." He gave her that smile of his, sending everything below her shoulders into supernova.

"So I hear."

He laughed. "Is that so? And who'd be telling you that?"

"I had a conversation with Cordelia something-or-other this afternoon. Apparently you were her first and she's never forgotten you."

"Oh good gracious! That was so long ago, we were both so young. She didn't upset you, did she?" He kissed her temple.

"Conall, if I was going to get upset each time I was confronted by a female who'd tasted a bit of what you've got under the hood, my God, I'd be upset all the damned time. But you're mine and everyone has been quite sweet about it so there's nothing to be upset over. Well, except for Ninane. Boy, you really dipped your wick in the crazy pussy with that one."

Wincing, he scrubbed his hands over his face. "It was just a few times. She was only trying to get information about Aoife anyway."

They cuddled together on the couch after she kicked her shoes off. "I need to clean up before we go to your family's for Brenna's party. But Conall, it wasn't *just* anything to her. You should have seen her face when she talked about you. It may have been to get close to you to get leverage on Aoife but it was more than that. She has a thing for you and she's been nursing it for a thousand years. You're very good in bed, but she's obsessed."

"You wouldn't lurk around for a thousand years if we broke it off tomorrow?" He massaged her shoulders.

"I'd kick your ass if you dumped me tomorrow. You'd still be limping in a thousand years."

"You're sexy when you threaten my life."

"Mmmmhmm. You remember that. You're all mine, Mr. macCormac. If Ninane tries to hurt you again, I'll put a hurt on her she won't forget. Well, until she dies because she is going down."

He sighed. "Haley, she's very powerful. I just think you should leave it to Riordan, me, my father, or Aoife to take her out."

She heard the fear in his voice.

"I don't have her magic, no. But she won't get away with what she's done. If I can, I'll let others take her down. But if I have no choice, if it's me or her. It'll be her. I mean that."

"There are men looking high and low for her, waiting for her to leave below. When she does, they'll take care of it and you can be free to come and go as you please. Until then, Irish witch, watch that ass of yours. I happen to like having sex with you very much. If something were to happen to you, I'd be forced to go out and charm another woman and you know how I hate all that work."

"Well, that's too bad. Because I need someone to scrub my back." She stood and cocked her head. "I suppose I'll have to go it alone."

His eyes lit and she ran for the stairs, with him hot on her trail.

It wasn't until long after midnight when they stumbled back home. The evening had been chilly but not overly so. Still a sense of foreboding skittered down Haley's spine just as she began to fall asleep against Conall.

Chapter Fourteen

Samhain Eve arrived and Conall avoided Haley all day. He knew she was angry with him for being so dead set against her leaving but it was the disappointment in her eyes he hated to see so much.

She'd connected with her grandmother via the scrying bowl and he'd heard the sadness in her voice even as he'd been relieved she wasn't going to fight him over it.

They'd have their own celebration in the *brugh* later on in the day at dusk. Theirs was a royal family and so their participation in festivals on high holidays was very important.

Brenna had informed him she'd seen Haley down at the ford in the river with their mother and Aoife. Riordan had been keeping a not-so-surreptitious eye on her but it didn't appear she'd bolt or do anything silly.

Conall joined them as the light began to fade. His siblings and their children, his cousins, aunts, uncles, Aoife and her husband Ciaran all stood in the center of the ford. Haley, dressed in finery of deep green with gold at the hems, stood next to him, holding his hand as Aoife and Ciaran lit the candles.

The other residents of the *brugh* gathered and tiny bits of paper floated on the air as they burned.

When at last the ritual was over, everyone moved to the

tables that lay heavy with food and drink and celebrated. Conall felt the thinness of the veil that kept the *sithein* separate from the human world, felt his magic surge against his skin.

It was the first Samhain in a thousand years he'd celebrated with his family, filled with hope and happiness.

In the still after the moon had set, Conall had undressed her quietly and made love to her with such tenderness it had brought tears to her eyes.

Despite being sad she couldn't spend the evening with her father's people, she did enjoy her first Samhain with Conall and as a Faerie.

But her dreams were unsettling and she opted to sleep in that next morning instead of going off to work. She hadn't taken a sick day in years so she might as well. No more mead in the moonlight with Conall, it left her with too big a hangover the next morning.

Conall had already left for work by the time Haley made herself a leisurely breakfast. Afterward, she dressed warmly and worked in the garden a while, needing to feel the earth in her hands and knowing the work would soothe.

Just as it neared time for Conall to return home, Haley stood and a deep pain sliced through her stomach. Confused, she stumbled, moving toward the back porch.

She shouted out, knowing Cormac had guards somewhere within hearing distance and suddenly she knew. The warding spell Conall had put at her parents' house. Something was very wrong.

She ran as fast as she could toward the gates. Shouts rang out behind her, one of them Riordan's. He was fast and as she reached the *sithein* gates he grabbed for her but she could not be delayed.

153

"My parents, damn you! There's something wrong. Don't you fucking try to stop me!"

He hesitated a moment and it was all she needed to sift once she hit the doorway.

Enraged, Conall burst through the *sithein* and sifted a spare two minutes after she'd gone. His father was with him. Riordan had already gone right after her, yelling at the guards to tell the others where they'd gone. He was going to kick her ass for breaking her promise to him.

She was risking her life for a stubbed toe or a...all thought froze when he landed in his in-laws' living room and the scent of blood and dark magic assailed him.

Then he heard Haley, or what he thought was Haley. The sound sent a shiver up his spine. He ran toward it, skidding in a pool of blood where she knelt, his brother's arms around her.

The scene made no sense to his eyes at first. In the background he heard Riordan speaking Gaelic to Haley, telling her to calm, to stop looking, to let him use his magic to help. She made small, feral sounds of grief that cut at him. He wanted to move to her but the energy in the room was thick and his eyes would not understand what he saw.

Blood everywhere. Signs of a struggle but it must have been fairly brief. *What* was that in the corner?

"In the name of all that is blessed, this is blasphemy. This...Riordan, get Haley out of here now!" Conall heard his father say it, felt his touch at his arm right as he figured out Ninane had done something to pull Haley's parents apart so that nothing was recognizable. Dark spells etched the walls in blood. The taint of what had been done hung heavy. This was a violation of all their laws, of the laws of magic. Ninane had taken a step she could not move back from.

"I won't leave!" Haley began to scream and it freed Conall from his horror as he rushed to her.

"We have to go, Haley. This is wrong. You are not safe here. Hear that? Aoife has sent people, my father has too. They have to clean it up. They will take care of your parents. I make my vow to you. Irish witch, you can't help now. Please, please come away." He kissed her softly, wanting to erase the devastation from her face.

"What is this?"

The crack of magic that came with the demand filled the room, biting his skin. Riordan paled as he and Conall shielded Haley between them. Conall turned to see Aoife but he'd never seen her this way.

Her hair, unbound and dark as night stood around her head, floating on her magic. She wore a breastplate, smeared in blood older than recorded human history. She was the warrior queen, manifested there.

"This cannot stand. She opened a gate and unleashed hell in this room." Aoife's voice had an eerie quality as her magic pushed the evil from the space. She was one of the oldest, one of the first, Conall wasn't sure there were any around who could stand against her and he saw why.

"This is my fault. Don't you see?" Haley's voice was small, choked with emotion.

Aoife's terrible rage ebbed away as the darkness fell from the space, leaving only sadness and desolation. She moved toward them and placed her lips to Haley's forehead.

"Sleep and be dreamless, child. This is not your fault."

Haley fought it, Conall saw how angry she was at having her will stolen but she couldn't hold it off long and she slumped against him.

"I've sent people to Maeve's. She's alive but there was an attack on her house last night. She didn't want to alarm anyone but they'd woven a spell, holding her there. They killed her animals, even her dog who'd been outside. She'd been trying to reach us or get out. Healers have taken her to her people where they can help her get her strength back. I've sent a demand to Dugan but haven't heard as yet. We will avenge this, Conall. This kind of magic breaks our most basic laws and she's taken human lives and left evidence of our existence.

"Take her home. She'll be angry when she wakes up. Send for me and I'll speak with her then. When Maeve feels up to it, she'll come to Haley or, and you're not going to like this part, she'll go to her. Her people will want to avenge this. I advise you now to accept that and find a way to make it work."

Conall remained silent. It was a battle he wasn't going to think about right then. He nodded his thanks to Aoife, looked to his father and once around the room and he and Riordan sifted back to the *sithein.*

Chapter Fifteen

Haley woke up, confused and feeling like she'd been hit by an eighteen wheeler.

"Haley? Honey, how are you feeling?"

She turned her head to see Conall's face and warmth filled her. Happiness. She loved that face, loved his voice.

But it fell away a moment later. When she saw his features, saw the concern there she began to remember.

Her hand moved to cover her mouth as bile rose. She scrambled out of bed and headed for the bathroom, Conall on her heels.

Afterward, he'd held her as he took a cool, wet washcloth to her face and neck, speaking soothingly in Gaelic to her.

The way Riordan had at her parents' house.

Her knees buckled as it all came to her in vivid color. All reds and violent splashes. The remains of her mother and father. Not together, not right.

She shook her head as madness clawed at her. Her brain couldn't accept it. It was *wrong*. What had done that to them? Strange sounds came from her. She wasn't sure how she made them or how to stop.

"Haley, come back to me, Irish witch."

Conall picked her up and settled them in bed, her body

curled into his as he rocked her, smoothing a hand over her hair.

"You'll do no good if you let yourself go. You have to hold on. For me. For you. For them. Fight it. I know it's hard. I know. But don't let her win."

"Why, Conall? Why would she do that? What did she do to them?" The insanity within her eased back, but it still felt like broken glass shifting around in her belly.

"I don't know. I wish I did. I wish there were answers, Haley, but there aren't any. I'm sorry. I'm so sorry."

"My grandmother!" She sat up on a gasp.

"She's well. Aoife sent people to her the instant we learned about your parents. She's with her tribe." After a brief hesitation, he told her about the spell and the attempt on Maeve.

"Where are my parents? Or what's left of them? I'll need to deal with the police, won't I? Their house. Their jobs and friends. What's going to happen?" The enormity of what Ninane had done hit her. She'd exposed them all.

"Aoife and my father stayed behind. We've been exposed. They'll have to fix it. Aoife used a great deal of magic to convince the authorities your parents died of carbon monoxide poisoning. You'll need to go back and deal with them. For now, they're under the belief you're out of the country, out of contact but will get with them as soon as possible. Your grandmother has made arrangements to ship their bodies to Ireland."

"I have to go to her. When will Dugan deliver Ninane to Aoife? Will you be the one to prosecute her?" If she stayed focused on tasks, the pain was just barely survivable.

He sighed. "Haley, Dugan won't deliver Ninane. He's refused. He says we have no proof it was her. He even blamed us saying we did it to put the blame on Ninane."

"Well, so I imagine we're at war now. I need to help. I'm sure Riordan will be someone in charge now. Your father too."

He remained silent long enough for her to push away from him and see the look on his face.

"What is going on?"

"We're not at war, Haley. Technically, Dugan is right. We don't have the proof it was Ninane other than basic common sense. We're working on the proof now. Aoife has magical scholars studying the marks on the walls. We'll get the proof."

"Are you telling me that fucking butcher who ripped my parents into pieces is going to get away with it? She's *free* right now? I know it was her who attacked me. What about that? Or do I not matter at all?"

"You do matter, Haley. This will not go unavenged, I make my solemn vow to you."

Haley turned to see Aoife standing in the doorway, looking very tired.

"So you said five months ago when Ninane tried to kill me. And yet, she was free enough to kill my parents and try to kill my grandmother."

"I cannot just storm in and take her. Even after that attack. There are rules. I'm sorry. You don't know how sorry I am but the rules keep us from war and they keep roughly a hundred thousand Fae from killing each other and humans too. I've demanded a trial. Dugan is dragging his feet. More now because he claims Ninane won't get a fair trial with this incident being blamed on her."

"Incident? My parents were in pieces! Their blood was everywhere. On the ceiling. What did she do to my mother to get her blood on the ceiling? I don't care about your rules. I don't care! You talk a good game and yet *nothing has happened* except I'm now without parents. Because of me. They're dead

159

because I came here." Haley's voice had reached screaming proportions, her head throbbed, her mouth tasted ashes, she felt nothing but rage.

"Sweetness, please calm down. You're only going to make yourself sick." Riordan came into the room, holding his hand out.

"But I'm alive to be sick. I'm alive here. Safe here. And my parents didn't have that option. I chose you people over them and it got them killed."

Aoife cocked her head. "I never had daughters. I have many nieces who I love very much. But you're important to me, like a daughter. I feel your pain. If I could risk all the *sitheins* under my rule to avenge your loss I would. But my blood is in my vow to the treaty. It controls my magic, it controls the safety of every *sithein* and all her residents as well as the below where Dugan rules. The magic holds because it's within us, within the ground, the mounds, the sky. If I break my vow without obeying the rules, it all crumbles and leaves everyone defenseless. We would not win even if I did break my vow. It would only speed our defeat and the Fae would have a king such as Dugan. If so, what happened to your parents would happen to millions of humans."

Haley didn't want to care about any of them. She didn't want to wait, didn't want to be patient.

Conall put his arms around her and she rested her head on his chest. "Haley, this is not your fault. Lady, how I wish I could make this better for you. I wish I could erase it and if it meant getting rid of our bond to save you from this, I would even though it would kill me to not have you. But that can't happen. We can't go back in time. You're here with me and I love you with all that I am. Your parents loved you and they loved their life as humans. Your father gave that up knowingly and gifted his immortality to you. Don't wish that away, it was his gift."

This man touched her deeply. She'd associated her bond with him as a reason for their murder, she realized. It must have hurt him but he put her first instead of his own feelings. She didn't wish away what she had with Conall. She couldn't imagine how gray and flat her world would be without loving him. Even through the pain of her loss, she knew that.

"I love you, Conall. I may not deserve your love or this bond but I'd never wish it away. I'm too selfish. Promise me she won't get away with this. Promise."

He let out a long breath and hugged her tight. "I love you too, even when you're stupid and say things like you don't deserve our bond. And you have my promise. The promise of our tribe."

When he said it, she believed it. Held on to it because it was all that held back the madness.

Conall paced as his wife stared at him through red-rimmed, determined eyes.

"Honey, I just think it's better for you to stay here."

He'd tried very hard to retain his calm as they argued. He knew she was upset and grief stricken. He wanted to respect that. He also knew she'd get combative if he raised his voice and he wasn't mad anyway. Just desperate to make this all right for her, desperate to ease the pain from her face.

"I know you do. You've said it about three dozen times and while I admire your restraint and the bland way you're keeping your voice lest I shatter into a million pieces and all, I'm going."

"Haley, your grandmother is safe and she'll come here, you know that. There's no reason to go and expose yourself."

"I'm not making an old woman come here after she's had

her last remaining child murdered. And they're my people too, as was my father. I want to be with them right now. I dealt with the cops and my parents' friends and employers. I have to plan a memorial there. People loved my parents, they should have a time when they can celebrate their lives. I'm even more determined to travel now. If I catch her outside her little zone of protection, I will kill her myself. Rules bedamned. I will kill her for what she's done. I'm done hiding."

"What does that mean?" He froze.

"It means I'm not going to hide in this hill anymore. I'm going out when I need to. I'm going to see my father's people. I'm going to plan a memorial for my parents. I'm meeting with their attorney so I can arrange to have the house sold and the proceeds will go to set up a scholarship program at the Foundation in their names. I won't let Ninane steal another second of my life."

"Haley, you're upset, I know that. But you saw what she did to them. She will do that to you if she gets the chance. I can't...I can't walk into a room and see you like that. Don't do this to me. Please." He got to his knees. "You want me to beg you? Because I will. Please don't do this. I love you. I need you and I can't survive without you."

She moved slowly, kneeling on the carpet in front of him. "I don't want you to beg. I know you're freaked. I am too. This is a lot of tough talk on my part. But I can't let her make me cower. I can't. It's like she's here all the time, governing my every action. Our every action. Because she makes us afraid. Well, she did this to me when I was safe tucked up here. Don't you see? There's no difference to her. She'll harm us no matter where we are."

"It's me she wants, Haley. I feel responsible. I am responsible. You're mine to protect."

"She does want you. But you're mine. She can't have you. And so you and I will work to take her down. The *rules* aren't going to help here, you know that."

What kind of crazy plan did his Irish witch have brewing in her head? "Haley, I don't like that look on your face. You're up to something."

She fell back to the carpet and looked up at him. Lady, she was beautiful, even with dark circles beneath her eyes and the clear stamp of loss on her face.

"Help me forget, Conall. Put your hands on me and help me forget."

He couldn't resist. Didn't want to resist. He always wanted her, but when he'd seen her kneeling, covered in blood, not knowing at first if it was hers, the need within him to touch her in the way only he could, had begun to build.

Standing, he bent to pick her up and put her on the bed gently.

"Free your hair."

The longing and desire in her voice wrecked him deep inside where everything was Haley. Her eyes went half-lidded when he removed the tie from his nape, letting his hair fall forward, casting them both in shadow as it curtained around their faces.

"I love you, Irish witch. More than I ever imagined it was possible to love anyone or anything. Let me ease you for a while."

Dipping his head, he kissed and licked along the creamy column of her neck, tasting the salt of her skin, the tang of her sadness.

"Conall, not gentle. Please. Hard and fast. Let yourself go. I want you to unleash what you hold back."

His hands trembled at her breasts where they'd been softly kneading. "Haley, are you sure?"

She took one of his hands and guided it to her pussy. She was hot and slick. "What do you think? Give it to me, Conall. Own me. Mark me. I need that tonight."

With an anguished cry, he sank his teeth into the upper swell of her left breast. Not hard enough to do damage, but enough to leave a mark. Her tremulous gasp let him know she was still with him so he slowly unharnessed his desire. Bit by bit. He'd give her what she needed, what he craved, but he wanted her to be with him every step of the way.

She arched, spreading her thighs wider, rolling her hips and he brushed his fingertips over her labia. Teasing, tantalizing but not giving her what she wanted just yet.

He took a nipple between his teeth, worrying it as he flicked it with his tongue. She writhed beneath him, the heat rising from her skin blanketing him.

Pulling back, he sat on his haunches and grinned when she opened her eyes and glared at him.

"On your knees, Haley. Facing away from me. Bend forward with your hands holding the headboard. I'm so glad you talked me into the new headboard." He chuckled.

She obeyed. Her ass tempted him and he caught the glistening pink of her pussy when she bent forward.

Moving closer, he bent and pressed his face to her, widening her thighs with his palms as he tasted her honey.

Her groan vibrated through her body, against his mouth as she grew more slick, her taste flooding him.

He licked and nuzzled, his hands at the top of her thighs holding her open. His fingers dug into her muscles, loving the way she felt, strong and feminine all at once. Tremors worked through her as she edged closer to climax.

Her breath shuddered as she gasped for more. His balls tightened against his body as he gave it to her, plunging his tongue into her gate as deeply as he could. Her inner walls, superheated and wet, clasped at him before he moved back to her clit.

When she exploded, it was so intense he felt it deep in his gut, her cry filling his senses.

He'd have made her come again, eaten and licked at her pussy until she fell asleep from exhaustion but for her whispered, "Please, fuck me."

Barely able to speak, Haley slurred her plea over her shoulder. She needed him inside her, needed his body behind and above hers.

She felt him kneel and position his cock at her gate but when he grabbed a handful of her hair to guide her where he wanted her, a soft moan broke from her lips.

"Fuck. Haley, you gushed that sweet honey all over my cock. Damn it, I love that. I love it when you're wet and creamy for me."

He pressed into her body with one easy thrust, burying himself balls deep.

Haley felt each stroke, every inch of his cock slicing into her body. Felt the way her pussy stretched, accommodated him. The ridge of the head lit nerve endings. She loved the slap, slap, slap sound of their bodies meeting as he sped up. Loved the scent of her body and his mingling in the air.

White-hot intensity rushed through her when he leaned down and first licked her shoulder and bit, licking again to soothe the sting. That he reined in such need for her and kept control turned her on more than just about anything. Except for when he loosed it and she felt it coursing between them. Felt his more feral nature running through him as he gripped her hair tight and fucked into her hard and fast.

His voice was rough as he whispered to her. Things both naughty and exquisitely gentle. Every touch, every word and sound he made filled in the cracks within her heart and soul. Knowing she was cherished, adored, desired and loved by this man made everything a bit more bearable.

"I'm going to finger your clit, Haley. I want to feel your pussy come around my cock."

He moved his hand to her, flicking a fingertip over her clit. Chuckling, he licked the shell of her ear and never lost his rhythm. "You're still wet from my mouth. I can still taste you."

Haley had to close her eyes as orgasm approached, welling around her, sucking her into his spell.

"Yes, Irish witch, give it to me then. You wanted me to mark you and so I have. As you've marked my very heart. I do own you but it's impossible for it to be one way. You own me too. Right now, your pussy is mine and I want you to come."

Unable to do much more than hold on to the headboard and whimper, she opened herself up and let the pleasure shoot through her, let orgasm take over as the flush of it moved over her skin.

He mumbled a curse and thrust deeply as a bone-deep groan shook his body along with his climax.

He stayed there for long moments afterward, still inside her, still half-hard. He swept gentle hands over her back and flanks as he whispered in Gaelic.

At last he pulled out, rolled off the bed and carried her to their bathroom where they showered and stole kisses. There was no need to speak.

Chapter Sixteen

"I know you feel guilty. But you're doing all you can." Conall watched his aunt as she paced. They'd just received more delay tactics from Dugan, refusing to hand over Ninane or any evidence they'd requested.

"She's one of my people, more than that, she's very special to me and she's suffering and I can't give her what she wants right now. I know she's angry with me, I don't blame her."

Conall softened as he heard the anguish in Aoife's voice. "Aunt, she's an honorable woman. She understands what it means to live for more than just yourself. Yes, she's hurting and who among us wouldn't be? But she realizes there's a big picture here and once you explained the nature of the vow that held the treaty together, she's able to see what the limitations are. She loves you. As do I."

"She's still planning to go to her grandmother."

He realized what her fears were. "Not for good. She's not rejecting the *Daoine*, nor you as her queen. But," he sighed, "loath as I am to admit it, she needs the comfort of her father's people too. They want to know her and they want to reach out right now."

"Riordan will accompany you along with Mal. I won't argue. I want guards with you at all times. Your magic is strong. She's a warrior, that's her path. Just bring her back to us. Both of you, safely. You and your brother will keep an eye on each other and Mal will keep you out of trouble. I think I'd love some great nieces or nephews from you two so be safe."

"She wants to leave this afternoon."

Riordan spoke up from his seat. "We'll sift directly from one of the side gates. We've got warding spells in place everywhere. We know we're being watched. But I believe Haley is right when she says we cannot allow Ninane to terrorize us from within and without as well. We will do our best but if we are engaged, Ninane had better best me because I will show no mercy."

"She deserves none. She's broken our laws and has exposed us to the humans. I've called for the other ruling Fae to come together. But you know how this goes. It'll take months to get everyone's attention. Dana is working very hard on this. Go on then. Send my condolences to Maeve and the rest of her people. Bring my girl home safe and you with her."

"Majesty," Mal spoke quietly, "if I may?"

Aoife nodded for him to continue.

"I believe there are Fae here in the *sithein* who are giving information to Ninane. Cormac is looking into it. I think we should keep our trip as quiet as we can."

Conall closed his eyes a moment. He'd had fleeting suspicions but the idea of someone he lived near, of someone who waved at him when he and Haley passed by giving information to Ninane to help her in this insanity made him ill.

"Of course." Aoife's mouth sat in a grim line. "This..." she paused, "...I have no words. It must end. We cannot allow this sickness to erode our community."

Haley looked at the three men with her. "If things weren't so awful, I'd be crowing about coming with my own harem."

Conall caressed the back of her neck for a moment, soothing her nerves. "Come then, Irish witch. Let's go see your grandmother and watch Riordan and Mal charm her."

Instead of a *sithein,* the traveling Fae lived in a sort of enchanted valley. It existed in a space between the human realm and Fae. To the normal eye, it was little more than a bend in the road, an open spot in the sky as they drove past on a seldom used backroad.

The way shimmered as they approached, recognizing Haley's magic and her blood tie to their tribe. They walked into the sky and instead a beautiful landscape revealed itself. Where the land outside had been very cold and a light dusting of snow had fallen, it felt like a crisp autumn day within the wards of the valley.

Guards posted at the front gates greeted them warmly as Haley caught sight of a group of people hustling toward them. Her grandmother, arm in arm with her great-grandmother in the lead.

"Welcome to you, Haley! Your people welcome you home. You and yours are always going to find a pint of ale and a warm bed here. Come now, let's get inside!" her great-grandmother said, with hugs and kisses for the group.

In the warmth of her great-grandmother's very large kitchen, Haley drank tea and ate scones while her grandmother told them what'd happened Samhain Eve when she'd been attacked and then trapped within her house, her magic repelled and unable to contact anyone.

They'd all cried as Haley managed to get out the story of finding her parents. Conall and Riordan had to break in a few times to fill in details and Haley appreciated both their support. Mal flirted relentlessly with her cousins and her great-grandmother, making everyone feel a little lighter in his own way.

But it wasn't lightened totally. There was much anger in the room. It stung Haley's skin, reacted with her own sense of futility and injustice over what had happened and the continuing calls for her to wait.

"And how do you feel about this, Haley? Will you wait inside the *sithein* until the needed evidence is found?" Maeve watched her granddaughter and Haley sighed.

"I don't know. I trust Aoife has justice in her heart. I believe her pledge to do everything she can. But she's called the other leaders of the Fae and she says it may take months, even years to get them all to agree on a place to meet much less to meet at all. I find it very frustrating to hear how angry the Fae are at how Ninane has broken these covenants but to be told to wait and wait seems at odds."

"You are only recently full-blooded Fae, Haley. To us, years are not the same as they are to humans. To an immortal, the passage of time is different." Riordan squeezed her hand.

"I understand that. But the fact is, humans are being threatened right now by Ninane's actions. They're not immortal. And neither are we. The Fae can die. My grandfather was murdered, so were my uncles. We can be killed and we can kill." Haley's frustration crested at the idea of losing so many in her family to murder.

"This loss will be avenged. Those below cannot open up the gates and bring that darkness to the human realm. They cannot murder using magic. They cannot murder our people and get away with it."

Haley looked up at her second cousin, Rhiannon, who'd spoken so vehemently. "And what do you propose?"

"You're being trained by Aoife, are you not?"

Haley nodded, feeling Conall tense up next to her.

"You know we descend from Macha. There are those of us good with animals, horses mainly, and those of us good on the battlefield. You're both, Auntie Maeve says. I am too. As are several others of our tribe. Take us with you back to your *sithein* or stay here and we shall train together. We are warriors. They've taken from us and we should not let this stand."

"Haley, you know I ache for you. But this is madness. Ninane is nearly as old as my mother. She's very powerful. You all did not see what Ninane unleashed on Haley's parents. You cannot stand against that kind of evil. Few can. I can only wonder at what the price Ninane paid was." Haley heard the fear in Conall's voice. He wasn't patronizing her and her relatives, it was the truth. Ninane *was* way more powerful than Haley, and whatever dark magic she'd used was beyond Haley's understanding.

And yet Haley had learned a few things of her own.

"I'm not arguing she's powerful, Conall. And I'm not arguing for us to rush out tomorrow and engage her. But I do know a declaration of vengeance comes with its own brand of power, something wilder and deeper than what Ninane has."

"I knew I shouldn't have encouraged you to work at the archives." Conall scrubbed his hands over his face.

"I agree with Rhiannon and Haley." Maeve stood. "I let someone steal my life from me. I only lived halfway. I've lost my mate and now all my children. Haley is mine and I will stand at her side with my magic to face Ninane. It is my right as Cian's mother. I swear vengeance."

Rhiannon stood forward and clasped Haley's wrist. Haley clasped Maeve's wrist and Helen, Maeve's sister and Rhiannon's mother, came forward and took Rhiannon's wrist. They formed a unit there and their intent began to hum in the room.

Haley looked at Conall, needing him to be all right with her path. It was a journey she needed to take to avenge her parents. She wanted him to accept it.

He stood staring at her for some time as she watched the war of emotions on his face. Finally, he nodded, kissing her temple. "Blessed be on this path, Haley. You're my mate, my wife and I will stand by you even as my heart trembles in fear. You are strong and righteous and I will aid you however I can." He paused. "Even if I want to tie you to our bed and never let you leave the house."

Riordan stood next to his brother and Mal joined them. The other members of Haley's family standing in the kitchen circled them as well.

"I swear vengeance with my sisters. No more shall she walk any realms. Her dark deeds will be avenged and justice done." Rhiannon spoke clearly and the humming of each woman's magic began to modulate, harmonizing in a sense.

Helen's voice joined the group. "I swear vengeance for my lost nephew and his wife. For my brother-in-law and those nephews lost in their childhood. I swear vengeance on behalf of a mother who will not live to hold her grandchildren."

"I swear vengeance. Ninane will have no shelter strong enough to save her from our righteous wrath." Haley took her blade in her free hand and sliced the inside of her elbow. She handed the blade to her grandmother, who did the same. As each woman opened her own vein, the other to her left took that blood and drew a sigil of unity and justice on the forehead of the woman next to her.

When Maeve drew hers, the circle sealed, the magic welled and the humming broke like a bell, clear and strong. Haley felt the magic tie them all together and in that moment, she understood Ninane could not stand against it. The magic they'd created there was older than the jealousy that brought out the darkness that'd killed her parents.

Righteous magic would defeat the darkness. They had to approach their path carefully but if they did, they would wipe Ninane's stain from the sky.

Back at the *sithein*, Conall walked along the edge of the pasture where Haley rode with her little cell of Amazon warriors and Aoife. Riordan walked at his side, scanning the area for threats even as they spoke.

"I've never felt anything so powerful before as I did in that kitchen. Your Haley will be a woman odes are written about. And her grandmother! Were she five hundred years younger and interested, I'd be wooing her into my bed right now."

Conall laughed but then his shoulders slumped again. "I hate this."

"I know. But you did the right thing in supporting her."

"There was no other choice. I love her. She's been wronged and I fear justice will be long in coming any other way."

"We will train them and help. Aoife is behind this plan totally, which heartens me. She believes in Haley's strength and her magic." Riordan stopped and they both watched the women work.

Conall loved the way Haley looked as she jumped off the horse, her braid whipping around, face set in a mask of concentration. Even as he feared for her, he appreciated her strength and prowess. Who'd have thought that saucy redhead who came into his office the year before would have turned out to be a warrior?

Then again, he was sure she hadn't imagined losing her parents and being terrorized by a jealous, psychotic, crazy Fae either.

After working outside for some time, the women headed back toward town. Maeve, Rhiannon and Helen were all staying in a bungalow just up the path from Haley and Conall and in the few short weeks they'd been in the *brugh* they'd begun to fit into life there very well. It made Conall so glad to see Haley and her grandmother growing so close and many of the Fae from the *brugh* had come to the memorial service for Haley's parents. There was a sense of community where there hadn't been for her before. He hated that it took a tragedy to build it, but he loved that it was there for her. For them.

"Irish witch, I've got to run down the administrative building and do a bit of work. I'll be back by dinner. We'll eat out back tonight, do you think?" He kissed the top of her head, breathing her in.

She hugged around his waist. "Mmm, you smell much better than I do, I'd bet. Sure. Dinner out back would be lovely. I'll be waiting for you so don't waste time gossiping with your friends."

He laughed when she winked, glad to see her humor returning.

"I wouldn't dare keep a beautiful woman waiting." He dipped his head and kissed her lips quickly before striding toward his offices, leaving the sound of feminine laughter in his wake.

Haley parted ways with the others and headed home for a shower. It was her turn to cook and with the chill in the air, something hearty was definitely in order.

Uh oh, what's this all about? Haley stopped at her front gate when she saw Aideen approaching.

Aideen smiled hesitantly when she reached her. "Haley, I

just wanted to talk to you. I'm glad to find you alone. I..." she paused and touched Haley's arm, "...I'm so terribly sorry about what happened to your parents. Truly. I can't imagine what you must be going through and I know I gave you my condolences already but I wanted to do it just you and me. Because I've been a right prat and I said things that I can't take back now with your mother gone. You don't know how much I regret saying all that stuff at the pub that night. How much I regret hurting you that way and being so disrespectful about your mother, who I *know* loved you very much."

Haley blinked back her surprise. Aideen had been gentler, less abrasive in the last months since that big blow up in the pub. But what surprised her so was the genuine manner Aideen spoke with.

"I...thank you. Truly, thank you very much, Aideen. It means a lot to me that you'd do this." And away from an audience so it wasn't for show either.

"I know we got off on the wrong foot and that's my fault. I'm not making excuses for it. I love my brother very much and losing him for so long was awful. But I got him back and well, anyway, you make him happy. He loves you and you love him and that's what matters. I wish I could take back what I've said but since I can't, I'd like it very much if we could start over. Do you think we could?"

It took courage and honor to reach out the way Aideen had. Haley was touched. "I think I'd like that very much."

Aideen hugged her quickly before stepping back. "Thank you. I guess I'll see you at lunch day after tomorrow. Tell Conall I said hello."

Haley could have asked her to dinner, Conall would have had puppies in his joy over it. But yeah, well she was going to have to opt out of an evening with Aideen at that point. Working their way toward civility was a good thing but it was a one step at a time sort of deal.

Ninane met with her contact over a dirty martini in a Manhattan bar. He sneered as he moved through the crowd and she wanted to laugh. She knew how much he hated humans, which is why she arranged to meet him in Manhattan to begin with.

"Fuck you," he growled as he sat down.

"I think not. Anyway, isn't your little *Daoine* girlfriend keeping you busy in that arena?" Quite a coup that one had been, but she wasn't going to make his ego any bigger than it already was.

"Look, there's some sort of action going on right now. Haley and some women from her grandmother's tribe are training with the queen."

"For how long?" Ninane tapped a blood-red nail against her glass.

"About a month now. Just shy."

"And you thought to tell me now? Instead of a month ago?"

"Look, do you really think a former human and her grandmother are a threat? My friend doesn't take it seriously, I don't think you should either. Your new *friends* have boosted your power, haven't they?" He looked at her, annoyed by her summons but fear lurked in his eyes.

And rightfully so. Even she held fear of what she'd unleashed in Berkeley that day. Still, the darkness of it coursed through her veins, melding with her even then. It was too late to be afraid.

"What are they up to? Do they think they can defeat me with their magic?" She laughed out loud at the very idea.

"Battle training, apparently."

Ninane relaxed and waved a hand. "Oh that. Yes, the human has been working with the queen since she arrived. Must keep the boredom at bay and also her hand close to Conall's family."

"You did a number on the grandmother's house, my friend thinks she's taken refuge in the *brugh* for safety's sake. The woman did grow up without contact with her people." He wrinkled his lip in disdain. "I doubt they're a threat to you."

"Of course they're not. But I want regular updates on the situation. I need to be able to get in and remove that threat. Dugan will back me when the time comes. But he's bound, just like the queen is, until then." The treaty bound all the reigning Fae who'd entered it into a non-aggression pact. Ninane got away with all she did because she didn't give him details and he didn't directly participate. She pushed as far as she could but until one of the signators was dead, the treaty was in effect. Once Aoife was out of the way, open warfare could be declared. And with the new power within Ninane, that *sithein* and all her inhabitants would be hers.

All she had to do was keep the man before her thinking she believed in his goals so the rogue Fae living outside the *sitheins* and enchanted spaces would follow her. And as he had a direct connection to the royal family in his bed, she knew what a valuable ally he was.

In truth, she didn't care about humans one way or the other. They served a purpose but she had no desire to live in their realm like he did. She had no desire to kill them all either although she didn't really care if they died tomorrow. What lay inside her moved restlessly at the idea of all that death.

"It's no chore to fuck her more often. Although it's hard for her to sneak away."

Lauren Dane

"Does she still see you as a noble revolutionary or have you told her you're helping the woman who stole Conall's soul?" The woman was a fool to not see the male before Ninane as the threat he was. Little matter though, her stupidity helped Ninane.

He laughed and shifted a bit in his seat. "She'll understand one day. For now, it suits my purposes for her to believe she's just a lover talking about her family. It would not be a good thing if she knew you were involved so keep quiet or that avenue will be closed off. She's not very bright but she's one of them and sees herself that way."

Ninane rolled her eyes and downed the rest of her drink. "I'm not stupid. Now, I'll be off. Enjoy your evening." And breaking their laws once more, she sifted away in full view of any humans watching.

But when she walked back into the long hallway leading to the below, Dugan waited for her, angry, she knew, he'd been put in a position to protect her.

"Where have you been? Or do I want to know?" he demanded as he fell into step beside her.

"Protecting your interests. The rest isn't relevant for you to know." She'd need him at least for a while once they took Haley out and then Aoife too. Once she took over, Dugan was irrelevant to her life.

"You've got some months before the rest of the ruling Fae gather to correct this problem. Once they do, I have no doubt I'll have to hand you over."

"Fine. It'll be handled by then." Ninane had no other choice. And there was no way she'd let some human bitch like Haley win. Haley needed to die and then Conall would be a wreck. People would turn on Aoife for not protecting her own and the crack in the foundation would be made. With this inside

178

informant Riley had, they'd get the key and Ninane and her little friends lurking in her gut would walk into that *brugh* and kill Aoife and declare the throne spoils of war.

Chapter Seventeen

Conall strolled through their front door, happy to know they were alone. All the togetherness with her family was wonderful but it left them less time for sex and he missed the spontaneity.

"Hello, sailor."

She waited for him in the living room. A fire crackled in the fireplace and a tray with appetizers sat on the low table in front of the couch along with two steaming mugs of chocolate.

"And what does a man do to deserve such bounty upon his return home?"

"He's you. We haven't had much alone time lately so I thought it would be good to hang out here, just me and you. Everyone we know understands to disturb us is to endure pain."

"I love you, Irish witch. You look beautiful you know. Laying there, your hair loose like a sunset. That green is pretty on you."

"Totally naked beneath the robe. I'm just sayin'."

He laughed and suddenly he stood there in nothing more than low slung pants.

He saw her breath hitch and it made him smile to see her react that way.

"God, you're hot. Come here and let me rub up on you a bit." She got to her knees on the couch and he joined her.

"Hello, missus. Care to have your way with me?" He leaned back into her as she began to massage his shoulders.

"At least four times." She kissed his shoulder, her tongue flicking out to taste his skin for just a moment. Long enough to send shivers down his spine. "You taste good."

"Feel free to lick any part of me you desire."

Her fingers kneaded tired muscles as he relaxed against her body.

"That's very nice."

"I like the way you feel against me like this. I like taking care of you. You've been very good to me. Thank you. I know you're freaked and I just wanted to tell you how much it means to me that you're with me."

As she spoke, she pressed kisses along his shoulders and ears.

"I love you. I want you to heal and be happy. I don't like you being in danger, I hate it in fact. But you have a journey and I'm trying very hard to respect it and be part of it. I can't say I'm totally comfortable, I'm not. The idea of you training for some sort of showdown with Ninane makes me crazy. I want to protect you because you are the most precious thing I've ever known." He turned, desperate for her to know how deeply he felt for her.

She watched him through those beautiful green eyes, listening, features soft with love. No one looked at him the way she did, even when she was angry it was there, her love.

"Do you know what you are to me?" he whispered, caressing her face.

She leaned into his touch. "Tell me."

"Everything." He shrugged. "It's really that simple. I'm twenty-five hundred years old. I've lived a long time. Nine hundred of those years I lived, being born over and over to a gray world. The only thing I had any glimmer of feeling for was someone finding those scrolls and freeing me. Until you walked into my office. Since then, you've been it. Nothing makes me feel like you do. No one makes me want to laugh, cry, howl at the moon like you do. Haley, no one looks at me the way you do. I'd do anything for you. Even let you risk your life because you *need* to avenge a great wrong."

A tear rolled down her cheek. He caught it with his fingers, bringing it to his tongue. It wasn't sorrow he tasted, but joy. Haley.

"Conall, I'm not so old. I'm not even thirty yet. And so I never had any great longing in my life other than to learn things. I love...loved, my family. I loved my job. But you came from nowhere and then you filled me up, filled the spaces I didn't know I had. You answered questions I didn't know I needed answering, hell I didn't know I had the questions to start with. I look at you the way I do because you're you. You love me and I never feel wanting with you. Well, I do, but not that kind." She laughed.

"I'm blessed to have you in my life. Blessed that you love me. So early in my existence and you're in it. No pining for that for millennia, no dating my way through hot Fae dude after hot Fae dude until I stumbled into the office of the most sexy intellectual I'd ever met. You know how much brains turn me on." Shivering, Haley leaned in and brushed her lips across his.

"You're the total package. I love you."

He pulled her to him, into his arms where she belonged.

"I believe you said you were naked beneath this robe?" He untied the sash, parting the silk and discovered she'd been telling the truth.

"God, I love that grin of yours. If you could bottle it, you'd rule the world," she said on a sigh as he traced the edge of the tribal markings on her side, from hip to just beneath her breast.

He waggled his brows and sat back, pulling her astride his lap facing him. He took his time, licking and nibbling her nipples. She was fire in his arms, her skin heating at his touch, her scent rising as her desire increased.

Tracing the pads of his fingers up each knob of her spine, he drank in the sight of her, the feel of her, knowing no other would ever see her this way.

She scratched her nails over his chest, against his nipples and he hissed with the sensation.

"Turn around and straddle me," he murmured against her breast.

"I don't want to." She arched into him, urging him on. Instead he pulled back and laughed.

"I promise you'll be happy with the outcome."

Sighing, she gave him a sexy pout but moved around, giving him her back. He drew the robe down, exposing the bare skin and the sexy curve of her spine. It was then he saw she'd realized he'd magicked away his pants and ground herself over him.

"Well *I'm* happy with the outcome, that much is true." He pushed her hair off to the side, loving the way her skin looked there in the firelight.

"Can I put you inside me?" Her voice was taut with need.

"Well first, I want you to finger your pussy and make yourself come while I watch. Then I'll fuck you."

"Watch?"

"Look in front of you, Haley."

Lauren Dane

She met his eyes in the reflection in the wall of windows looking out over the valley below.

In the glass, he watched as her eyes slid partway closed and she caught her bottom lip between her teeth.

He rested against the back of the couch and watched as she caressed herself, her hands gliding over her breasts as she rolled her hips, stroking the full, wet, superheated surface of her pussy over his cock.

Like a goddess she rode him, one hand sliding down to her clit, frequently sliding over the head of his cock as she ground into him.

Her movements, once smooth, began to grow choppy, erratic as she rained honey over his cock. Her breath shortened until she arched back with a cry and came.

When she did, he lifted her a bit and thrust into her deeply, feeling the clutch and clasp of her inner walls around him as she continued to orgasm while he began to stroke into her pussy.

He loved this angle, watching her in the windows, seeing the reflection of his cock entering and retreating from her body, the enticing sway of her breasts, the way her fingers dug into her thighs as she began to undulate to get him deeper.

Her body had changed in the near year he'd seen her naked on a regular basis. She'd been fit before but now she was harder, battle ready. Her upper arms were well toned and muscled, as were her thighs. He loved the contrast of that with the softness of her breasts and the way her hair hung past her ass. All contradictions, his woman.

And later, when they lay against one another, tucked into bed, he hoped for a lot more moments of peace but feared there were more moments of grief to come.

184

Haley looked up through the skylight and watched the light change as dawn approached. She got up quietly and headed downstairs to make coffee. She wanted to work through something that'd been niggling at her for months now.

She'd been pouring milk into the mug when Conall came up behind her, pulling her into a hug.

"Morning, beautiful. Why are you up so early?"

Before she could answer, a knock sounded on the door. Conall tossed her the robe she'd left upstairs. "Here. That's Riordan and I think he'd be distracted to see you all naked and tousled so very early. Oh and you've got some love bites on your back and arse." He winked and she snorted while putting the robe on, belting it tightly.

A few moments later, her two favorite men came into the kitchen where she'd seated herself with coffee and toast. She nodded toward the counter. "Coffee is done. Bread's on the counter for toast if you like. Fruit and cereal in the pantry."

"I love that you have human food here. Makes me feel a bit homesick for the human realm." Riordan bent to kiss her cheek before grabbing the pot and pouring a cup of coffee for himself and Conall.

"Not that I don't enjoy seeing such a bounty of handsome first thing in the morning and all, but what brings you here?" She knew he must have done that little spell thing Conall often did with his family and sometimes her, just a little mental Post-it note to announce something.

"I saw the light as I passed. I've been out for a run." He sat at the table, across from Haley and Conall.

"You were just about to tell me why you were up so early, Irish witch." Conall sipped his coffee, wrinkled his nose and instead, conjured up some tea.

"Something's been bugging me for months now. Well a few

things but firstly, do you think someone within the *sithein* is giving Ninane information?"

"Yes. Yes I do. We've had our suspicions for a while and Riordan and my father are working on it. Aoife knows and it's her belief as well. I'm sorry I didn't talk to you about it. It felt like you had enough on your plate and I didn't want you suspecting anyone unnecessarily." Conall leaned up on an elbow and kissed her lazily. "Why? Has something happened?"

"No. It's just that it seemed such a coincidence when Ninane knew I'd be here or leaving. She could have watched all the gates but as some of them shift often, it would be difficult to always know. And she seems to know things about me, where my grandmother lived, where my parents lived."

"She chose Samhain because the veil between worlds was thinnest and she could move easier. I don't know if she knew exactly where your parents were at first though because of the delay. She didn't attack them at dusk on Samhain Eve or midnight. But she did choose dawn. Either someone here gave her the information about your parents or she was able to get it from whatever she discovered at your gran's house. I'm sorry." Riordan buttered some toast as he spoke.

Haley looked at Conall and shook her head. "Why? First of all, I want you to tell me stuff. Stop sparing me this way. I know you're doing it to protect me but really, just tell me. And I don't get why anyone here would want to hurt me and help someone who tried to kill you. It feels like there's something we aren't seeing."

"Like what? I have some ideas but I want to hear yours before I say anything." Conall drew circles on her wrist with a fingertip.

"This isn't just Ninane. It's more than whatever beef she has with you. I mean, if she did what she did to you in the first place, she couldn't have been working alone, right? What was her aim? To get rid of Aoife. But then what? Did she say what her plans were?"

"She wanted me to tell her about Aoife's movements and also the source of her magic that held her to the treaty. I don't know what her plans were if she proved successful though. I've always wondered."

Riordan snorted. "Me too. And you're not alone in wondering, Haley. I keep wondering—why? What would she get out of it? Who was behind her?"

"It couldn't have been Dugan, not openly. He's as bound to the treaty as Aoife is. He could help her indirectly, he's a craven bastard." Conall shrugged.

"Who else would want to harm Aoife? This tribe? And who within this tribe would want to harm it? I've looked through the archives, I know there are rogue Fae. Fae who aren't affiliated with the tribes."

"Yes, and they'd love to get control over one of the tribes. But I'm not sure they're organized enough to do anything. Not anything important. From what we can tell, they want to live in the human realm and not hide our magic," Conall said.

"Well, some hate humans and want to kill them all. Some feel like hiding from humans—when we're the more powerful race—is weak of us so we should rule them. And others just want to live in houses and drive cars and also have magic at their disposal. It's hard to unify with so many different goals." Riordan peeled an apple, halving it and putting some on Haley's plate.

"I think part of the solution is to get at what the hell is going on here. And then I think we need to sucker that cow Ninane into a trap and be done with her forever."

Conall laughed and hugged her with one arm. "Irish witch,

who'd have thought you'd be so bloodthirsty? It's very sexy."

"She needs to die. I'm quite happy to be the one to make that happen."

"We'll deal with her, I promise you, Haley." Riordan looked dangerous as he told her that. "By the way, Aideen went with me to the firing range yesterday evening. She's working very hard. Thank you for giving her another chance."

"Everyone deserves a second chance, I suppose. We aren't best friends or anything, but she's trying and I'm trying. She's family and she's acting like it. That counts for a lot with me."

Conall kissed her temple. Haley knew how much it meant to him that his sister and wife were getting along. Even if Aideen had merely been tolerable, Haley would have been willing to heal the rift. But more than tolerable, Riordan was right, she was working hard. Aideen adored her brother, Haley happened to agree with her that Conall was worthy of adoration. It was a start.

Riley looked down at his lover—his informant—he corrected himself. Beautiful and fragile and she had no real idea what she did. The little things she told him weren't anything she did with the intent to fuck over her family or her people. She just talked to him about her life and he listened, encouraging her to share, all the while using her ignorance against her. He planned to keep it that way. Even if she was a tool for him to get what he wanted, he didn't think it necessary to harm her emotionally if he didn't have to.

He tried to tell himself it was because one didn't misuse their toys but he knew it crept into territory beyond that. Ninane would kill him if he blew her off or exposed her in any manner. Not just him but his people and the woman lying beneath him, writhing as she came around his cock. It suited everyone to have Ninane think this woman beneath him was an informant for his cause instead of a woman he was developing some rather deep feelings for.

So many pieces in play, he realized just how ridiculously complicated the situation had become because of that bitch Ninane. Riley just wanted some peace. To stop hiding the nature he was so proud of. And now he was involved in something above his head. What Ninane had done to Conall macCormac's human in-laws broke laws even he agreed with.

Too late for second thoughts. He'd play his part and hope he was alive at the end.

Chapter Eighteen

"We have to flush out whoever is feeding information to Ninane. I'm sorry it hurts you but we can't just let this person continue to harm the tribe." Haley looked at Conall as he tapped his pen against the tabletop.

They were in a strategy meeting with his father, Aoife, Haley's team and Riordan. Everyone in the room could be trusted but beyond that, it made Conall sick at heart to think everyone else was suspect.

"Haley, why put yourself purposely in danger? We can do this another way." Conall nearly growled as he rubbed his temples trying to ease his frustration.

"She's right, Conall. I'm sorry, I know you're worried and I am too. But something important is going to get someone to move. This is all focused on her. She's the one who has to expose herself. It's common sense." Cormac shrugged but emotion filled his eyes. He cared about his daughter-in-law too, Conall knew.

Conall shot up out of his chair. "Why are we asking my wife to take all the risks here? Damn it! She's done nothing wrong and I'm sick of her being the one to take all the hits."

"I know. I know it's unfair and I wish there was another way. I wish I could do it myself. Haley is one of my people to protect and I've done a poor job of it. No one knows that more than I do." Aoife's voice was thick with emotion.

Haley reached out and took Aoife's hand. "There's enough blame flying around. You're the queen, you're nearly immortal but you're not a superhero. Stop trying to be. I know I was mad at you after my parents...after we found them. But I don't blame you for that. I just want to catch the leaker and I want this over with. You can't do this. You're bound by the treaty. But I'm not. I'm doing this. Conall, honey, I love how protective you are of me but there's no other way."

Sighing explosively, Conall slammed his fist to the table with a curse. "Fine. Damn it, fine. But I'm going to be there and you're not going to argue."

His minx of a wife smiled up at him charmingly. "Of course. Now Aoife has to leave because we're going to discuss particulars."

Aoife leaned down and kissed the top of Haley's head. "I do love you."

"Right back atcha." Haley winked and Conall stifled a growl. How dare she be flip when she was taking her life into her own hands this way?

Aoife left and they got back to work. Haley would make a trip out of the *sithein* and expose herself to the outside world. Rhiannon would be in place with her bow, Riordan would be in position with a sniper rifle, Maeve with her magic along with Conall. Helen would also set up a sniper position. It was more a fishing expedition than an ambush for Ninane. They'd float the story about Haley leaving but just to a few people to narrow down the field of possible suspects. Including his own family and their friends.

That night they had people over. It was winter solstice and Christmas approached so Haley thought a gathering would be the perfect cover and also a way to celebrate even in the midst of the stress.

All he hoped was Ninane didn't show up at the meeting spot two days later because if she did, it meant someone he loved had betrayed them and he couldn't bear the thought.

His parents, Aoife, Ciaran, Mal, Aideen along with Rhona, Dev, Brenna and Patrick, Riordan and the group Conall had begun to think of as Haley's Warriors—her grandmother, great-aunt and cousin—were all there. They decided to keep it small. If no one showed, they'd move to another group. They knew Ninane would be motivated by the need to move before the ruling Fae gathered to hear her case. Conall just hoped it made her desperate and stupid and not desperate and dangerous.

Haley laughed, despite the danger in the air, she was such a part of his family. So strong, his woman. And good.

"I hate this," he murmured to Riordan. "I hate looking around this room and wondering if my own blood is trying to kill my wife."

"I know. But it has to happen and we can hope all Haley does in two days is go shopping." Riordan sipped his champagne and looked around the room at everyone.

The information was planted quietly and subtly. Riordan was quite good at this stuff, Conall realized not for the first time. They ate and celebrated and he hoped against hope this was all a mistake.

Two days later, Haley dressed warmly and headed to the gates. The rest of her team had left earlier to take up positions to cover her. Conall would leave via another gate but for now he had to walk her there in plain view and pretend he wasn't going to vomit at what a totally stupid thing his heart was going to do.

"Be safe and don't spend too much money." He winked at

Haley and she laughed, kissing him quickly. They'd made love just minutes earlier, fevered and animalistic, needing to connect. He licked his lips, tasting her.

"I'll see you soon. Thank you for trusting me to take this trip. You know how important it is to me to shop for the holidays."

And she was gone.

Agonizingly slow, he walked back to their home and used the spell Aoife had given him so he was able to sift directly from their living room to his spot overlooking Fifth Avenue in Manhattan where Haley would be shopping.

Haley sifted into a quiet spot where no one would notice and walked out of the subway tunnels and up onto the street. Fifth Avenue. Even with the danger around her, it felt good to be out and about without a retinue of people flanking her, frowning at her for wanting to dawdle just a bit.

She'd have preferred to choose an isolated spot and just be done with Ninane by killing her there, but they hadn't been able to explain that away and they wanted to take this slowly, gauge Ninane's new strength before striking.

And in truth, she hoped like hell Ninane didn't show. No matter what Conall thought, Haley didn't want anyone in her living room two nights before to be involved.

She used enough of a diffusion spell when she sifted that a casual observer wouldn't know where she went. Only someone who knew ahead of time could have given Ninane the information.

She shopped, buying a lovely pair of boots for Aoife and a scarf for Dana and she'd just walked back onto the street when she felt it. Sickening, dark and for want of a better word, evil.

"Fancy seeing you here."

Haley looked into Ninane's smirking face and saw something move behind her eyes. Something dark and oh so very wrong.

"I'd ask how your family was, but well, I hear not so good."

Rage coursed through Haley. "You bitch. You're going down for what you did to my parents. And no one will remember you in six months." She used the spell Dana had given her to gauge Ninane's power and it wasn't good. Something utterly foreign and not Fae at all leeched from Ninane's aura.

"Oh, so deluded. You're the one they won't remember. I'd love to kill you right here in the middle of the street." Ninane flicked a wrist and Haley felt the sting on her cheek. Her fingertips slid against blood but she ignored the fear.

"What is your problem anyway? You tried to kill Conall and now you're trying to kill me? Why? It's not like you can have the throne or even that I have a damned thing to do with it. Why are you so obsessed with me?" Haley wanted to know, damn it.

"You can't have what's meant to be mine," Ninane snarled. "Conall. My place in the tribe. It's mine, not yours."

"Not like I'm an expert or anything, but if you want a dude you show him your tits! Oh wait, you did but that didn't work. Still, fer fuck's sake, you cursed him and stripped him of his soul for nearly a millennia! Men tend to get a bit pissy about stuff like that. Aphrodisiac? Not so much."

"Be a smartass while you can still draw breath. But when you're dead, I'll have Conall and my rightful place."

"You can suckit, you fucking crazy psycho bitch! He's not yours. He's *mine*. All mine and I like that very much. I'm not just rolling over for the likes of you." Haley's anger made the hair on the back of her neck rise.

They'd begun to draw a crowd and Haley could practically see Conall's face in her mind. She knew he'd be angrier than all get out that she didn't get away right when she saw Ninane but she wanted answers and now she had a few.

Now the point would be to make Ninane keep underestimating her. It'd be painful but worth it in the end.

"I hear you're shite in bed anyway. You'd think after a few thousand years, you'd know how to suck cock." Haley raised a brow, inwardly bracing for Ninane's strike.

When it came, Haley half expected someone to shoot Ninane as she felt the slice along her side and the warmth of her blood oozed from it. She didn't make any effort to deflect the strike, let the bitch think she couldn't.

Five minutes later, Haley could barely stand and she was losing blood at an alarming rate. She had to get out of there quickly. Thank goodness the crowd began to push in and during the chaos, Haley was able to slip away and sift directly back home.

She collapsed at the foot of the stairs, having to crawl her way up, leaving a bloody mess in her wake. She'd gotten about halfway up when she heard Conall bellowing her name as he thundered up the stairs toward her.

He looked around, paling at the blood smeared over the stairs and all over her body. Panic threatened his sight, going gray at the edges. So much blood! Damn the woman, she lived to torment him. Gently, he scooped her up and headed into the bathroom. "What the bloody hell did you think you were doing, Haley?" His energy went into not shaking or screaming at her for being so reckless. Instead, he magicked her naked and turned on the taps in the shower one-handed while keeping her against him.

More voices downstairs as the others showed up, not having the spell to get back directly.

"I've got her in here. She's naked which means stay the hell out, Riordan," Conall called out while never taking his eyes from his wife or the dozens of bloody stripes angrily marking her flesh through Ninane's magic. "Haley, you're losing a lot of blood."

"Let me clean up. It's worse than it looks. I'm already beginning to heal. There's some of that healing paste crap left over from my attack before. It's in one of the drawers. I need to get the stink of her off me." Haley's voice shook as he let her stand. Gripping his arm, she moved under the spray and his heart broke. She shouldn't have to deal with this.

"Damn you. Irish witch, why did you push her so far?" he asked as he gently massaged shampoo through her hair, trying to ignore the pink water going down the drain. She leaned back into him.

"I had to make her think I was weak. She has to underestimate me. We need her to think defeating me will be easy. And she's totally obsessed with you."

Nausea roiled through him. He'd heard the way Ninane had spoken of him and her belief he'd go to her after she'd dispatched Haley. As if he'd ever leave this woman's side for another.

"This is my fault. I never should have fucked her. Never should have flirted with her."

Haley turned as she rinsed, pressing a kiss to his chest. "Don't be stupid. She's batshit crazy, Conall. You're good in bed, I'll give you that, but your dick didn't make her into a loon. She was already there. She cursed you. She would have killed you if she could. Whatever defense mechanism she had to try and make that okay made her nutty."

She stepped out, the blood still seeping from the wounds. She grabbed his arm as she nearly lost balance and he growled, sitting her down with a towel. "Don't move. Let's get this salve on you. Magical wounds don't heal as easy as those made with objects like blades."

The rest of what they'd learned that day hung in the air as he worked. But she didn't say it. He loved her even more for it.

"I used that spell your mother taught me to gauge power. Ninane is wrong. There's something very unnatural about her. She was loopy before but now there's a darkness inside her. Literally. I've never felt anything like it. Cold. Evil. When I looked into her eyes it was like there was something in there with her." Haley shivered.

Conall wiped his hands and finished bandaging her up. At least the bleeding had stopped and she seemed to be less pale.

"We'll talk to my mother about it, and give a bit of an explanation to Aoife. I think she's opened herself to something not at all of this world. It makes her much more dangerous."

"I know. Go and talk to them while I get changed. My grandmother will be worried."

He kissed her, pulling her into his arms. "Nothing is going to happen to you, Haley. I refuse to let anyone take you from me." He magicked some clothes for her and swung her up into his arms. "You're going to eat and rest for now while we talk to the others. I don't want you out of my sight. I need to know you're all right."

"I know. I do and it gives me strength." She snuggled into him and his heart rate finally began to slow after the near stroke level it'd been at since they sifted earlier.

He'd been up in his perch with Maeve, listening to the exchange. His heart had broken to see Ninane approach, knowing someone in that room two nights before had betrayed them. And then Ninane had started spouting all that crazy stuff.

When she'd begun to attack Haley, Maeve had gripped his arm and they'd watched, agonized as they saw the blood. Haley's shoulders had begun to droop. He would have sifted there to her but Riordan shook his head hard, even as he'd watched through the scope on the sniper rifle.

When he'd seen Haley back off and disappear he'd come right home. The sight of the blood on the stairs and his love crawling to get to the bathroom had nearly undone him.

One thing was crystal clear, Ninane would die.

Haley looked up to see several anxious faces relax when they saw her come into the room with Conall.

"Thank goodness you're all right." Her grandmother had made a little nest for her on the couch and Conall deposited her there, tucking her in. A cup of tea was thrust into her hand and Rhiannon's magic began to envelop her, warm and reassuring. Rhy was something of a healer and immediately, Haley began to feel less lightheaded.

"Now, drink this. It's some broth."

Haley handed the empty tea cup to Conall and took the mug from her grandmother. Just afterward, Dana came into the house, face drawn into a worried mask.

"Haley, honey, are you well? You're so pale!" Her mother-in-law fell to her knees and put a hand to Haley's cheek. "Did that bitch harm you? Oh goddess, she did. The mark on your face...I can't believe this whole thing."

"She'll be all right, Dana. Haley is a strong one. Conall put some of the salve on her wounds and Rhiannon worked some healing on her. She's drinking broth and resting." Her grandmother patted Dana's arm and drew her away to sit across the low table.

"I guess this means we've got a spy in the family. How did it get to this?" Dana buried her face in her hands and Haley felt so bad for them all. Wondered if in some way they'd come to resent her for this whole mess.

Cormac shouldered his way into the house with Aoife, and Haley told them everything that Ninane had said. Aoife worked her magic on Haley and the wounds disappeared. Haley supposed that was why she was queen.

"I'm going to go work. I've got things to do and Ciaran would love to see me at home from time to time. Haley, sweetness, you'll probably feel tired in a bit, I used a lot of magic on you. There's a darkness in what she touched you with. Taint. I'll mention it when I demand Dugan turn her over to us. I doubt that'll happen, but just in case he grows a conscience it would be something to bring up."

Aoife nodded at Cormac and left the house.

Riordan looked straight at Haley and grinned. "You're as fucking insane as Ninane is! You kick ass, Haley."

Conall actually growled. "Why are you encouraging her?"

Riordan's grin relaxed as he looked back to Conall. "She did what had to be done. Now Ninane thinks she's weak but our little redhead is anything but. I know it nearly gave you a heart attack, but you did the right thing too. When the time comes, Conall, you'll be instrumental. You're the focus here, Haley is just the path to you. But until then, you're going to have to let Haley run out front and I admire you for letting that happen."

Conall sighed and shook his head. "You're all the death of me. When do we get to the part when I'll be instrumental?"

"We've got to figure out who is leaking information as well you know. I hate to say it but Aideen is looking like an obvious choice here. Patrick maybe but he hasn't left the *sithein* in a week. Brenna loves Haley. We know it's not Aoife or Ciaran, Mom or Dad. Rhona? She's Haley's best friend but I suppose anything is possible. Dev?" Riordan began to pace.

"If it was Dev, Haley would be dead. He's no nonsense and highly skilled." Cormac leaned over and kissed the top of Haley's head.

This was her family and no one had the right to endanger that.

"Who all left in the last two days?"

"Everyone but Patrick," Cormac replied. "We had everyone watched. It's a busy time of year of course. No one was gone for more than a few hours though."

"Why would anyone help Ninane? That's what I don't get. I truly don't think it's Aideen." Haley tried to sit and Conall gently pushed her back, narrowing his eyes. "Aideen adores Conall and well, she and I aren't best friends or anything but I don't think she'd hate me enough to want me dead. And Rhona? I can't even think it! She's had plenty of opportunities to harm me if she wanted to. Brenna? Come on! She's one of the people who's welcomed me the most. I don't know, Dev isn't overtly friendly to me but he's doing the mattress mambo with Rhona. Could he be sleeping with her and plotting to kill me with a woman who cursed his friend? Is everyone just faking it then? I don't know what the hell to believe!"

Everyone goggled at her.

"What? They are? You're kidding!" Riordan sat on the table, leaning toward Haley.

"Huh?"

"Rhona and Dev are an item?"

"This is what you're excited about? And duh! Isn't it

obvious the way he looks at her every time she enters a room? And the way they try to avoid each other when they're at the same function? Oh and she's my best friend so I get details. That I won't share so get that look off your face, Riordan. I thought everyone knew."

"Obviously not." Riordan snorted.

"In any case, let's move on," Cormac interrupted. "We can do both. Work on finding out who's been giving information to Ninane and also plan on taking her down."

"Should we wait to see if Dugan hands her over for trial?" Haley asked, resting her head against Conall's side.

"Not going to happen. He won't hand her over. Even with what happened today. My guess is, he'll hold off until he can't anymore. That will take months at the very least and with someone on the inside helping, I'm less and less convinced of how secure we are should Ninane push. We can take her, she's not a god. But..."

"We don't want to expose everyone in this *brugh* to the violence she'd bring. And with whatever she's pulled into herself, we don't know what she'll expose us to. We can't take the chance." Haley felt in her gut they had to move and move decisively and quickly. The longer they delayed, the longer Ninane would have to hurt people.

"I looked into her and saw something so evil." Haley shuddered. "She has to be stopped. Whatever we plan, let's keep it between the people in this room. That way the leaker has nothing to share. What's most important is stopping Ninane. Then we can figure out who's betraying us. And why."

Conall let out a long, explosive breath. Haley knew he understood the gravity of the situation. Knew they were right and truth be told, she wasn't sure how she'd be reacting in his place. She understood just how much he trusted and loved her to let her go ahead with this plan.

"I'm very lucky, you know. Thank you." She kissed his shoulder.

He looked surprised a moment and then his face softened. "You've got my number, don't you?"

She laughed, pressing into him more.

"I love you. I hate this. But it has to be done so let's do this."

Chapter Nineteen

"Ninane!"

She flinched, hearing Dugan's angry bellow thundering down the hall.

"What is it now?" she replied, trying to remain calm. The darkness within her smoothed out her nerves, ate the angst and the fear like it was candy.

"I told you to leave it alone! And now I get a demanded summons because you've yet again attacked Conall's wife. In public! On a street in the middle of the day, in front of humans. I cannot protect you when you're so reckless and stupid."

His face darkened with rage.

"Who says I did this?"

"Aoife and Haley. The healer saw the wounds on her. Aoife tells me she's concerned for my safety because you've been possessed by darkness." He eyed her carefully.

"They can't prove it was me. It's her word against mine and she's trying to make me look bad to get you to surrender me." She sidled up to him. "I'm not that stupid, Dugan. You know I realize how tenuous your situation is by keeping me here. And I do appreciate it so very much."

For a moment he looked into her eyes and relaxed as she stroked her fingertips over his cock through his clothing. And then he recoiled, moving away from her quickly.

"What lies within you, Ninane? What have you opened yourself up to?"

Damn.

"Nothing, Dugan. You're letting Aoife and her accusations affect you. It's just me. Come to bed, let me show you the multiple reasons for keeping me safe." She sent him her most seductive smile.

"You've endangered us all, Ninane. You're compromised. What is within you is wrong. Unnatural. Out of balance and it will destroy everything." He moved toward the doors and she knew he meant to turn her over to the *Daoine*. That couldn't happen. She had plans!

She sighed. "I didn't want to have to do this. It complicates things and I have enough complications just now. You forced me to play my hand, Dugan."

He threw a magical shield up to stop her but the essence within her slid through it and she watched, idly, as it clouded around him. The dark mist turned red and then nothing remained but a puddle.

She magicked herself a bucket of water and a mop. She hated to clean but she couldn't very well leave a puddle of Dugan on her bedroom floor.

It was ten days later when Ninane finally managed to leave and arrange to meet with Riley. She'd been looking all over the place for the source of the magic that held Dugan to the treaty but hadn't been successful.

His lieutenant, a man who shared her bed often enough to be controlled into helping her keep up the façade that Dugan was still alive, had also helped but they hadn't found it.

Until they did, the treaty couldn't be broken by the tribe as a whole. Ninane could still do her level best to sabotage Aoife and the *Daoine* and to get rid of that bitch Haley to take what was rightfully Ninane's.

When she ruled them, things would be different.

She stalked through Central Park and saw him on a bench, wrapped up against the chill. Without preamble, she sat next to him with a sigh. "What do you have for me? I can't wait around forever."

"She's leaving to do some event in a little over two weeks." Riley gave her the details. "She wants to do some blessing at the site with her grandmother so they're going a few hours before the ribbon cutting to do it alone. Conall is staying behind, some sort of crap to prove he trusts her ability to protect herself."

"Even better. Imagine the guilt he'll feel! I'll have men with me. She's a weakling and we can incapacitate Maeve easily enough. I want this over. We move, kidnap Haley, kill Maeve. We'll ransom Haley to Aoife, kill anyone who tries to save the bitch and then when I get the throne, I'll kill the queen, the human bitch and take over. You of course, can live wherever you like. We won't be protecting these weak shells anymore."

He didn't meet her eyes, but stared forward. "What about Dugan?"

"He's not a problem. I'm already ruling the under as it is. Once Aoife gives me her source of magic holding her to the treaty and she's dead, I'll rule them too. The treaty will be broken and there will be others who back me. There won't be enough of them to deal with the humans. Delicious chaos will reign. As long as your people give me allegiance, you can do whatever you wish."

"Does Haley or the grandmother know you were responsible for killing the grandfather and the uncles all those years before with Dugan?"

"I'd forgotten about that." Ninane laughed. Oh, how long ago it had been. Dugan's brother had been infatuated with Maeve. They'd arrived at the traveling camp and slaughtered everyone but mother and the smallest child. In fact, now that she thought about it, Ninane had been shocked at how bloodthirsty and fierce Maeve had been when she struck back, killing Dugan's brother before sifting away. It'd happened some time before Aoife had banished Ninane from the *Daoine* but it had done its job and cemented her place with Dugan's tribe.

"She doesn't know, I don't think. But won't it be delicious to tell her right before she dies." It would be wonderful, Maeve's grief would be a meal for the darkness within.

Ninane detected a slight wince from Riley and wondered if he was getting soft.

"You need to spare my friend."

Ninane laughed. Apparently he was. "Oh you've developed a care for the little betrayer! Isn't that sweet."

"She doesn't know! And I like to fuck her and I want to continue that. She'll be mine after this. She'll live with me out here. You'll have my people at your back when you get ready to take over. Do you need them at the site when you take Haley?"

"I think not. She's a speck. I nearly bled her out on a crowded street two weeks ago and she did nothing. She freezes up when she's scared. She's mine and I'll deal with her. I'll tell you when I need you so don't ignore my call."

She sifted away, laughing.

Chapter Twenty

Haley sat, back against the wall, sharpening the edge of her blade. She watched the others as they worked and trained, watched the looks of concentration and felt the intent in the air.

It wasn't like she'd planned to grow up and be a warrior. Or that she'd ever imagined herself sitting in a room while plotting to kill another living being.

At the same time, she'd distanced herself from her friends and that sucked too. Not knowing who the leak was distressed her more than Ninane did.

They had plans to let Ninane ambush her in a week. They'd given the information about Haley's trip to the dedication ceremony to everyone suspected of being the leak. Now it was all just about getting ready and waiting.

She hated waiting. Haley just wanted to be done. In two days it would be officially a year since she had freed Conall from the curse. The last twelve months had been filled with incredible highs and lows. All that was the most wonderful in her life smack dab against all that was the worst in her life.

But it was her life and despite all the pain, she'd found her place in the *brugh*, with Conall and with her family. Funny, but in a way, facing all the pain and getting through while continuing to move forward had helped her not just survive but to grow and find her path too.

Three to five hours a day, every day, they drilled and worked out with swords, blades, hand-to-hand, magic and firearms. Haley wasn't a freaking SEAL like Riordan was, but she was confident in her ability and Ninane would go down because that's what had to happen. That bitch had harmed her family for the last time.

At the hot springs, Rhona, Brenna and Aideen were there. Haley tried not to let it affect her, only one of them was the leak but it was hard to think someone hated her enough to want her dead, enough to collude with the person who'd harmed Conall so much.

Ninane had stolen that from her too, her trust in people. No matter what, it would be over in a week and they'd pick up the pieces one way or another.

As she walked back toward home, Rhona caught up to her. "Wait a second, Haley!"

She turned and saw her friend, smiling before she could think about it.

"So, you want to tell me why you've been so odd the last three weeks? This has something to do with Ninane, doesn't it?" Rhona looked her over.

"I'm fine. I'm just tired and you know, it's crazy around here. I get distracted. I promise in a few weeks it'll be better."

Rhona grabbed Haley's upper arms. "Tell me. I'm your best friend. I can help you. I'm worried about you."

Haley kissed Rhona's cheek. "I'm fine. I promise. Really, it's just being very tired and stressed."

When she looked at Rhona, Haley simply knew it wasn't her. It couldn't be, damn it. "It'll all be over soon. I swear."

"You're up to something. Let me help you." Rhona's voice lowered but Haley noticed she kept her posture casual so anyone who saw them wouldn't think they were talking about anything more important than sex or clothes.

"I am. But you can't. No one can."

"Take her out, Haley. There's no other way to be safe. You know where I am if you need me." Rhona squeezed her hand and walked away.

Conall had to work later than usual, writing the summons for Ninane to be turned over to the *Daoine*. They hadn't heard from Dugan at all in the last several weeks. Not even his usual smug denials.

More troubling, Aoife had reported an odd feeling each time she'd tried to connect with him, a sort of disconnect. His assistant had just told her Dugan would answer when he was ready and cut her off.

Conall had left a note at home for Haley, telling her he'd be late. He hated being away from her, especially as the time for the ambush approached. But he wanted to expend every legal avenue he could.

In the end, he knew they had one option and that was Ninane's death. But he was a man of reason, which meant he could understand that but he also had to pursue all sources of remedy. He'd feel entirely justified when Ninane died, but it would be knowing he'd done the right thing every step of the way.

He was a man of honor as well. Just because Ninane was a ruthless murderer, didn't mean he couldn't take the high road *and* make sure she didn't take another breath to harm him or his again.

"Hey there, handsome. Got time for a game of interrogate the prisoner?"

He turned, smiling at her voice. The light of his universe stood there. "Why hello there, Irish witch."

With a grin, she bounded into his lap, throwing her arms and legs around him in an embrace. "I missed you today."

"Me as well. I'm nearly done. I was just putting everything away and getting ready to leave."

"Oh good. Because I want to have sex with you."

Haley loved the way his face changed as she flirted with him. His eyes darkened, lips parted, his breath caught just a moment before one regal brow rose.

She hadn't really planned to say that, but when she'd come upon him he'd been sitting at his desk looking so very smart and lawyerly it made her all tingly. Smart men had always been her weakness and the one currently grinding himself into her pussy was the smartest man she knew. Well spoken but fun loving and very dirty when he needed to be. Passionate. Mmm. Conall.

He stood and she wrapped her legs around his waist, holding on to his shoulders.

"Oh it's like that, is it? Well I can work with that." The thickness of his brogue sent shivers of delight through her.

Strong too. He held her up, pressing her to the wall as he kissed her hard, his tongue dipping into her mouth to taste and tease. Spinning, he plopped her ass down on the top of his desk and sat. Her shirt was rent in two as he feasted on her breasts first through her bra and then skin to mouth when he yanked the sports bra she'd had on, down to expose her nipples.

"Door," she managed to gasp.

With a flick of his wrist, the door slammed. He towered over her. One arm banded around her shoulders, he kissed her while he lowered her to the desk, her legs still hanging off the edge.

Clever fingers made very quick work of her pants and she heard the sound of silk ripping and saw the flutter of the material when he tossed her panties to the side.

Her skin tingled everywhere he touched, anticipating what he'd do next. She waited, loving the way he feasted on her, body and soul.

"So. Fucking. Hot," he mumbled right before he pressed his lips to her pussy, making her cry out and arch up to meet him.

He ate at her, taking long, slow torturous licks and nips. Haley was pretty sure she'd never been so wet in her life. Her thighs trembled and her muscles burned. She tightened, needing to come but he wouldn't let her.

She reached down, pulling him closer, holding his head against her body as he did unbelievably delicious things to her clit with the tip of his tongue while his fingers dipped, tickled and pressed in all the right, and a few very wrong, but oh so good, places.

"Conall, if you don't let me come right now I'm going to ki— oh hell yes!"

Orgasm, long awaited but totally worth it, rushed through her as her head hit his desk. She'd worry about how much it hurt later but right then, she had no words for how hot he looked as he stood, lips still glossy with her honey. His chest heaved as he pulled his pants open and his cock spilled out.

She scrambled to sit, wanting to touch, to see. Stepping forward, he pushed her thighs very wide and fed his cock into her pussy.

Entranced, she watched as he pushed deep into her, labia parting to admit him, flushed and swollen. How hot was that? Watching as he pulled back, the deep flushed stalk of him slick with her.

"It's beautiful, isn't it? I love to watch my cock fucking into your pussy. Love how your body makes way for me every damned time like a miracle."

"I was made for you, Conall." She didn't need to say anything else, that's what it was.

He leaned forward, burying his face in her neck as he increased his speed.

The girth of him kept her wide, holding her open as he thrust and pulled out, thrust and pulled out. The weight of his balls slapped against her ass until he got closer and she knew they drew tight against his body. She held him, gripping his shoulders, wrapping her calves around his ass to take him deeper, to open herself to whatever he wanted to deliver.

All that filled the air, other than the scent of sex, were the sounds of lovemaking. Sighs, grunts, whispered entreaties, his chuckled or growled responses and finally her gasp as he reached around, plumped her clit between his fingers and brought her off, followed shortly by his hoarse cry.

He handed her the handkerchief from his pocket and she laughed, cleaning herself up. "Such a gentleman."

"You came first, didn't you? I'm a total gentleman."

"Well, if that's the criteria, yes, you're so gentlemanly you should be knighted by the queen."

Her legs were shaky but she managed to get her pants back on. The shirt was a loss but magic was handy for wardrobe malfunctions and as they left the building and walked out into the frosty night air, they were reasonably respectable but hurried back for another round at home.

"It's not Rhona, Conall." Haley drank her juice and looked out the windows in the kitchen.

"Okay."

She turned to face him. "Okay?"

"I trust your feeling on this. For what it's worth, I don't think it's Rhona either." He tucked a bit of hair back behind her ear, kissing her softly.

"If it's not her, it's one of your sisters or a dear friend!"

He nodded.

"How can you be so calm about this?" She stood and began to pace.

"What else can I be, Haley? Every one of them has left the *sithein* since we told them about you and Maeve being alone in a few days' time. We know one of them is betraying us. I don't know who it could be or why. There's no way to know unless I interrogate them all and then it could get back to Ninane that we know. We'll lose the upper hand." He caught her as she paced, and hauled her to his chest.

"You are the most important thing in the world to me. This has to be over. It's gone on far too long. We will end it and then we will know who the leak is and we'll have to deal with that knowledge. But we can't change what it is. I've lived long enough to know wishing something wasn't true won't make it so."

"I hate that it has to hurt you so much."

He closed his eyes a moment. "What I hate is that you're in danger. Every time we part, even just for the day, my heart feels like it's going to burst out of my chest. I fear for you. But you make me strong enough to get through because this is the only way. When this is over, you and I are off on a very long vacation somewhere sunny. We will lie on the beach drinking something fruity and alcoholic and I will worship your body multiple times a day."

"You're full of it. But I wouldn't want you any other way. I just hope you don't blame me when this is over."

He narrowed his eyes. "We've had this discussion before. You don't think much of me to imagine such a thing. I blame you for what you do. I don't blame you for what others do. I'm not an idiot." He let go and moved away.

She hooked a foot around his ankle to trip him and rolled atop him with a grin. "Okay. I'm sorry. You're right. This is all very EMO and stuff so let's stop it or I'll have to drag out my old Cure CDs and light lots of candles. Maybe I'll write you terribly soppy love poetry about how my heart is bleeding. I'll draw bleeding hearts in the margins of my lined paper and everything."

At his blank look she sighed. "EMO as in emotional. You know all those boy bands where they wear black eyeliner and whine about break ups and stuff? Good Lord, didn't they have teenage girls in Ireland? I mean, I know you didn't have any real emotions when you were a teen but the girls would only have thought it made you hotter. All remote and cool. I bet every folder owned by a girl in your high school had, *Mary loves Conall* written on it. I would have. My Pee Chee folder would have had *Mrs. Haley Shaunessey* scribbled all over it. I'd have pretended to hate you while I sat in my room, listened to Morrissey and wrote bad poetry about you."

"For some reason, I think if I'd known you as a teen, you'd have been able to stir me even then. Did you have such a lovely chest when you were a teen?"

She found herself on her back as he rolled her over. He might be okay with her being a warrior, but sexually, he was in charge. She didn't mind that one bit either.

"You're a pervert. I like that about you. I'll tell you all about what I was like in high school, well I'll pretend I wasn't obsessed with math and language and robots. Maybe I'll even put on some very tight sweaters for you and we can park sometime. I never went parking. I may even let you get to third base."

"Third base?"

She leaned up and whispered in his ear and he laughed, taking her all the way around the field right there in their hallway.

Chapter Twenty-One

The morning of what might be the last day of Haley's life dawned gray. She'd been awake for several hours, just staring into the familiar space around her, listening to the man she loved breathe, shift, wake up and go back to sleep. She knew his dreams were troubled, wished she could make it better. Hoped that when the sun went down, he'd have better dreams ahead.

Strangely, Haley wasn't afraid. She was tired. Weary of the intrigue. Weary of having to suspect people, of being so careful, of worrying over the fragility of those she loved. Hating to see the look in her mother-in-law's eyes, knowing she resented, even in some subconscious way, Haley's presence because one of her family had turned against them all.

It would be over, one way or another, in a matter of hours.

She'd said everything she needed to say to Conall the night before. Spilling her most intimate hopes and fears. He'd listened, never interrupting, just holding her and stroking a hand over her hair. He loved her, she loved him. That's all there was to it.

That love was a nice, warm weight in her soul as she sent off a prayer to her parents, wherever they were. For guidance and strength to see this through.

She got up and showered. When she walked into their bedroom, Conall, saying nothing, hauled her to him and plundered her mouth with a kiss designed to mark her to her soul.

She felt the desperation in his touch.

The evening before, they'd had a last, quiet meeting. Had broken bread, worked some magic, Aoife had blessed their weapons and they'd vowed to see the sun set, alive and well, the next day.

They'd stayed up until the wee hours, needing to make love again and again. Each time they'd finished she'd thought, *if I die in the morning, I'll have had this perfection while I lived.*

As Haley left through their front door, Conall snuck out the back, choosing to leave through one of the side gates with stealth. Her grandmother hailed her with a wave, and she and Haley headed for the front gate of the *sithein* in plain sight. They took their time, letting the others get into place. Rhiannon, Riordan and Helen had all left an hour before. Cormac and Conall would have sifted by now and would be in place.

Dev wished them a good morning and called out that he'd see them in the pub later that night. Haley hoped that was true. Hoped he and Rhona would be celebrating and not weeping or in jail for their crimes.

Once outside in the human air, Haley turned to her grandmother and kissed her. "Ready to rock and roll, Gran?"

"I'm ready, darling."

They sifted to the field where the groundbreaking would be sometime after noon that day. A building with her parents' names on it. It felt like the right thing to do.

They began to bless the site. But unbeknownst to Ninane,

they'd also set up spells of protection and anchoring the day before. No one, not even that darkness within Ninane, could remove any of their group from the site without permission. Ninane wouldn't be kidnapping anyone that day.

Ninane came up over the hill and looked down into the meadow. The land had been cleared and marked for construction so her view was clear.

"You should just kill her from here and be done with it," Bert, Dugan's—her—lieutenant, whispered in her ear.

She wanted to be close enough to capture the energy from all that death and pain, to feed on the power and the magic. She couldn't do that from up there.

"I plan to look into her eyes when I kill her." She stood. "Come along then."

The two women didn't look surprised to see her, which took Ninane aback slightly.

"Hello there. Come to pay your respects?" Haley stood and the magic around her shimmered.

Ninane laughed. "Is that customary when someone is going to die then?"

"You don't usually give them when you're the one dying though, Ninane."

Haley moved quicker than Ninane anticipated and the edge of a blade sliced through her arm.

She jumped back with a cry and motioned her men forward.

Just then, others came from all around and Ninane realized she was the one who'd been ambushed.

Brenna pushed the door open and saw Riley there. She

smiled. He thought he was so tough but really, he was so lovely beneath that exterior.

"I don't have a lot of time. I'm going with my family to a groundbreaking in a few hours. I wanted to stop in and tell you something, though. I've spoken with Patrick and told him I wanted to leave him. It was hard at first but I think we worked it through. He's angry and hurt and my family will all be very upset and disappointed in me. We'll work through it for the children, who'll be very upset I know. But I've done it and you and I can make a future now."

She sat next to him but he looked pale. Panic unfurled.

"You did mean it when you said you wanted me to leave Patrick and be with you, right?"

He turned. "Yes. But..." he sighed, "...nothing. Stay here with me then. Wile away the hours since you no longer have to sneak around. We'll face your family later. It's not going to be easy to get them to accept me."

"It won't. I'll be honest. We've been wrong you know. But they'll see how much you love me and I love you. In time they'll come around. And I wish I could wile away time with you today but my sister-in-law is doing something very important and I want to be there. I told you about it, the groundbreaking thing. She went early with her grandmother but I'm going to pop in to help with the blessing of the place. I want her to know our family supports her too."

She kissed him and moved to stand but he caught her to him and held on.

"Don't go, Brenna. Please."

"What is it?" His voice, the way he held on so tight alarmed her.

"I just want you with me."

"Stop this! You're scaring me. Tell me what's going on, Riley. You're not yourself today. Or tell me later, I've got to go. I mean it."

She began to sift but he called out her name. "Listen to me! It's a trap."

That stopped her.

In halting words, he told her how he'd been giving the information she'd shared about her family, about Haley, to Ninane.

"Did you ever love me? Was this all an act?" Grief made her numb. She'd not only betrayed her husband, but she'd betrayed her family.

"At first it's why I sought you out. Ninane promised to help my people, let us break free and live in the human realm openly. But then I did grow to love you. I swear." He got to his knees. "I swear to you. I've made arrangements to keep you safe. You have to stay here."

"I have to go and warn them!"

Brenna sifted away from his flat to the site of the groundbreaking.

And right smack in the middle of a battle.

Conall saw his sister sift right into the open field and shouted her name. He couldn't sift her away because of the anchor spell.

Thank the Lady she fell to the ground and a bolt of magic just barely missed her. He saw Haley inching toward her and then he saw the discussion ensue, watched Haley pale. She slapped Brenna and he realized who the leak was.

"I didn't mean it! I didn't do it on purpose!" Brenna screamed as Haley kept her sheltered by her body.

Ninane casually tossed magic at Haley, who couldn't get close enough to use a weapon.

"He took the things I said, just stupid stuff about my daily life, he took them and gave them to her. I didn't know. I'm sorry. Please believe me, I didn't know!"

Haley turned and screamed in Brenna's face. For a moment all movement stopped at the sound, rage, grief, frustration, love, fear all rolled into one.

"My parents were ripped apart because you cheated on your husband with the wrong guy! It's not enough for my grandmother to have lost her husband and other children, you had to be sure she lost the last living one too? Couldn't you have kept your mouth shut while your legs were open?"

Ninane's delighted laughter cut through the air. "Oh and about that. Nice to meet you, Riley has told me so much about you, Brenna. I've promised to keep you alive for him. But I'd nearly forgotten, so thank you for reminding me. Maeve, I had the pleasure of being part of the raid on your home when your husband and sons were killed. Such a bloody day." Ninane's voice was sing-song and Conall moved quickly, pressing with his magic, watching the reaction on Maeve's face.

Reaching them as movement began again, he shoved Brenna down and threw a shield up in front of Maeve just in time as Ninane tossed out a killing stroke with her magic.

"I'm sorry. Haley, we'll deal with Brenna when this is over but keep your fucking concentration or I will kick your pretty ass. Kill this bitch and then we can deal with everything else," Conall growled at his wife who blinked hard and the resolve came back to her features again.

Pushing the pain down, Haley spun to avoid a sword stroke by one of Ninane's people.

221

Another burst of magic and a dark-headed Fae male ran toward them shouting Brenna's name.

"Riley! Get out of here!" Brenna screamed and Haley stifled the urge to drive a fist into Brenna's face.

"Hey, asshole, you killed my parents. I'd say prepare to die but that's been done. Until I can kill you, get the fuck out of my way and take your whore with you. I can't protect her right now," Haley yelled back over her shoulder.

An arrow whizzed by and caught Ninane's shoulder. A bloom of dark red stained the shirt she wore.

"Nice shot, Rhy!" Haley called out.

Ninane looked toward where Rhiannon was perched in a nearby tree, her attention focused on reloading. Haley watched, horrified as Ninane sent a bolt of magic at her cousin. Cormac battled two attackers and it left Rhiannon vulnerable.

Haley charged Ninane and instead was charged from the side. She heard two things, Conall screaming and the rip of tendons in her shoulder. Warm wetness soaked her as she was hauled to her feet by her husband who looked every inch the wild Celtic warrior.

"Took 'em out for you, my dear. Now let's deal with Ninane."

Haley saw her cousin had jumped from the tree at the last minute and was safe before turning back to face Ninane.

"It ends now. You've broken our laws and I suspect you're behind the reason Dugan hasn't responded to any of our missives over the last three weeks." Riordan moved toward them as he yelled.

Ninane waved that away and when she did, magic shot toward Maeve. Brenna jumped up and pushed her out of the way. With a cry, Riley did the same, taking the full hit of magic and crumpling.

"Young love, so tedious." Ninane's laugh sent shivers up Haley's spine.

Every time they'd try to move in closer, Ninane darted out of their reach with strange, not even Fae speed. Her voice continued to change, to deepen and echo.

Her men fell around her as the *Daoine* took them out but Ninane continued to fight.

"Haley, take your grandmother and the rest of your women home. Take Brenna and her man too. We'll clean up here," Cormac said gently.

Haley shook him off. "I am not leaving until this is over. Save your daughter yourself. I won't be doing it."

"You're very strong, Haley. It's the vengeance magic. We hadn't even thought of that. Very old. As old as us even." Ninane's movements were fluid, totally not human, or Fae, at all.

"First of all, you're totally creeping me out with the horror movie hopping around. Second of all, why are you using the royal *we*?"

Ninane stood, alone in the field, all her men down. Arms stretched up toward the sky a darkness seeped from her, misting around her form.

"Dear Lady, it cannot be," Conall murmured, grabbing Haley's arm and yanking her back.

But it was her bad arm and she cried out, stumbling.

As if time turned to honey, Haley watched as Conall turned, his face changed into a cold mask. He jumped up, wrenched the sword from her hand and charged at Ninane, who'd aimed magic at Haley's prone form.

Maeve screamed out, aiming magic at Ninane, Cormac roared and charged and Riordan stepped in front of Haley to shield her, calmly pointed a nasty-looking handgun toward Ninane, waiting for a shot.

Rhiannon managed to help Haley up as they watched Conall and his father rush the thing that had once been Ninane.

"Take the head!" Riley was able to yell from his place on the ground where Brenna held him.

Suddenly, a chorus filled the field. People shouting to take the head over and over and Haley caught one clear glimpse of Ninane's face through the mist as she understood she couldn't hold off the magic and the physical attack at once.

Conall planted his feet, twisted and swung the heavy broadsword in an arc, sending Ninane's head, the hair looking so pale in the early morning sunshine, through the air.

The body slumped.

"Shield yourselves!" Maeve screamed as the dark mist began to swarm like angry wasps.

Haley shielded as it brushed across her, wanting in. The cold of it burned her skin but it finally went away in search of other quarry. No one on that field left alive would invite it in that day.

Conall collapsed next to her, pulling her against him, breathing her in. "Alive. Thank the Lady, you're alive. Let's get the hell out of here. I want to go home."

"You saved me. You saved me and you avenged my parents." Haley pressed her face into his neck, holding her arm as she wept.

"You're mine. I'll always get your back."

Chapter Twenty-Two

Haley saw her grandmother, great-aunt and cousin back through the gates and toward home three days later. She still wore a sling to hold her shoulder in place. Aoife and the healers had mended the tears but it would be a while before she was totally shipshape again so she wore the sling to keep the arm immobile while she healed.

It felt odd to stand in the open without fear and Haley wasn't sure she'd ever get rid of the feeling at the back of her neck from when the darkness touched her.

But Ninane was dead and a new king had taken Dugan's place. After they'd declared him deceased, the treaty had transferred through the magic of the other Fae rulers to the new king. Those in the below had a lot of work to do to rebuild their tribe and Haley almost felt sorry for them.

They'd paid restitution to Maeve and the Traveling Folk for the murder of Haley's grandfather and all her uncles and father. Haley had taken her share and put it into the program at the Foundation in the form of a fellowship in robotics. Her dad would have liked that.

Aoife was in negotiations with Riley's group of rogue Fae. Haley stayed far away from that entire business. On one hand, she knew Brenna did not intend to betray her with her pillow talk. She'd just been sharing her day to day life with her boyfriend. On the other hand, that carelessness had gotten Haley's parents tortured and murdered. Haley's children would not have grandparents on their mother's side, and even in the aftermath, Brenna had stuck up for Riley and stayed at his side. Riley, who knew what he was doing and did it anyway.

So much unresolved emotion there. Haley's relationship with Dana had cooled a bit, which made Haley deeply sad. Dana was distraught by what her daughter had done, but she was her child. Haley understood it but it hurt anyway. Because Haley wasn't in a place where she could get past it. Didn't think she'd ever be. She was relieved that Brenna hadn't been knowingly colluding with Riley, for the sake of Conall and his family, but it didn't bring her parents back.

Conall hadn't pushed, understanding Haley's feelings in a way that made her ache. He took her side over his sister's. Knew his sister was wrong and while Haley knew he loved Brenna and had forgiven her, he always put Haley's feelings first and that meant everything to her.

Speaking of that sexy Fae devil, he stood just on the other side of the gates, leaning against a tree and giving her that wicked grin of his.

"Hello, Irish witch. Care to have a pint with me in the pub? Rhona and Dev are going to join us. Riordan is in a right funk now that Rhiannon has left." He pulled her into a hug when she got within reach and she breathed him in, letting him hold her and make things okay.

"He should have made a damned move for heaven's sake. She tossed herself in his face for months. Men. I suppose a beer would be nice if you're buying." She tipped her head back to look at him. Knowing she'd be able to do that for thousands of years pushed all the gray clouds of the Brenna business far away.

He kissed her, smiling into her eyes. "I'll always buy you a beer. It makes you very easy. And I love easy."

"Good God but you're full of it." She laughed, feeling better than she had in a very long time.

"I've got more for you later. Once I've got you full of alcohol and we get home. It'll be all dark. Maybe you can put on a tight sweater for me."

"If you're good."

"I'll throw in a bag of crisps."

She laughed again. "That might even get you to third base."

"Well then! I think they have a new flavor, might that get me a peek at what's beneath your panties?" he asked while they approached the door to the pub.

"It would." She walked inside and turned to him. "If I was wearing any."

"Minx!" He swatted her ass as he laughed.

"I love you, Conall."

"The feeling is entirely mutual."

About the Author

To learn more about Lauren Dane, please visit www.laurendane.com. Send an email to Lauren at lauren@laurendane.com or stop by her message board to join in the fun with other readers as well. www.laurendane.com/messageboard

What do you do when you've got a hillbilly tiger by the tail? Or maybe the question should be: what wouldn't you do...

Here Kitty, Kitty
© 2007 Shelly Laurenston

Nikolai Vorislav likes his single life just as it is. Simple, relaxing and quiet. What he doesn't need is some foul-mouthed Texan hellcat living in his house, eating his food, flirting with his idiot brothers and shooting holes in his home with his granddaddy's gun. But those long legs, dark eyes and lethal tongue are making Nik insane and he fears he may be caught in the sexiest animal trap ever.

Angelina Santiago doesn't know how she got from Texas to North Carolina in a night or how she ended up in some hillbilly tiger's house wearing only a sheet. What she does know is that she doesn't like good ol' boys with slow, sexy drawls who can't seem to stop rubbing up against her. Yet in order to protect her friends, Angie has to stay with a cat who seems hellbent on finding all sorts of delicious ways to make her purr.

Available now in ebook from Samhain Publishing.

A trained assassin…a man even the deadliest of warriors fear.
To cross him is foolish. To steal his heart is pure madness.

A View to a Kill
© *2007 Mandy M. Roth*
Book two in King of Prey series.

Sachin, head advisor to the king of the Accipitridae realm, has been forced to put his trips to Earth on hold. He's not been honest with himself or King Kabril about his need to visit the primitive planet. The king thinks him to be a womanizer, out to bed as many human females as possible.

In truth, a woman he should have been able to woo with little to no effort—his mate—has found someone else to fill that void in her life. She wasn't supposed to be on Earth. She wasn't supposed to be human. And she sure the hell wasn't supposed to agree to marry another man while Sachin was away.

Sachin must make a choice, give up the one woman he knows to be his true mate and let her live in ignorant bliss of what walks among her people, or fight for what's his, taking it at all costs. A trained assassin…a man even the deadliest of warriors fear. To cross him is foolish. To steal his heart is pure madness.

Available now in ebook from Samhain Publishing.

GET IT NOW

MyBookStoreAndMore.com
GREAT EBOOKS, GREAT DEALS . . . AND MORE!

Don't wait to run to the bookstore down the street, or
waste time shopping online at one of the "big boys." Now,
all your favorite Samhain authors are all in one place—at
MyBookStoreAndMore.com. Stop by today and discover
great deals on Samhain—and a whole lot more!

Samhain
Publishing, Ltd

WWW.SAMHAINPUBLISHING.COM

GREAT cheap fun

Discover eBooks!

THE FASTEST WAY TO GET THE HOTTEST NAMES

Get your favorite authors on your favorite reader, long before they're out in print! Ebooks from Samhain go wherever you go, and work with whatever you carry—Palm, PDF, Mobi, and more.

Samhain
publishing
Ltd

WWW.SAMHAINPUBLISHING.COM